Liberty Falls

A Holinight Novella

Lee Jacquot

A HOLINIGHT NOVELLA

LIBERTY
Falls

LEE JACQUOT

This is a work of fiction. Names, characters, businesses, places, and incidents, as well as resemblance to actual persons, living or dead, is purely coincidental.

Copyright © 2022 by Lee Jacquot

All rights reserved.

No part of this book may be reproduced in any form or by any electronic or mechanical means, including information storage and retrieval systems, without written permission from the author, except for the use of brief quotations in a book review.

Cover Design: Ria O'Donnell at Graphic Escapist

Editing & Proofreading: Mackenzie at NiceGirlNaughtyEdits

Ellie McLove at My Brother's Editor

A Quick Note From the Author

Liberty Falls is a standalone novella in the Holinights series. None of these books need to be read in order.

It is a sweet, steamy, and fun read intended for mature audiences of legal adulthood age as it includes explicit consensual sexual scenes. It should NOT be used as a guide for kinks or a BDSM relationship.

The author is not liable for any attachments formed to the MCs nor the sudden desire to have someone drip massage wax on your best parts.

Reader discretion is advised.

Here's to the one handed, multitasking, need a break from the angst and into the smut abyss warriors.

Aria
CHAPTER ONE

Men. I swear that three-letter word is enough to envoke a thousand different emotions from just a handful of women.

For me, the majority of the time, it's annoyance. Whether it's from some type of superiority complex, the lack of common courtesy, or the way that they can never seem to find *that spot* again, even after I just said *not* to move.

Don't get me wrong, I'm not anti-men or anything. But heaven help me, some men—particularly the asshole captain over at the Liberty Falls Fire Station—make me glad I have ol' faithful in my top drawer. Because somehow, even without proof, I *know* he's responsible for my current predicament.

A fire rolls through my gut as I ignore the sharp bite of my nails digging into my palm.

"I'm sorry, Chief Castillo. I'm not sure how this happened."

My heated gaze flashes back to the mayor's timid secretary, who's doing her best to deliver the bad news. She tucks a blonde strand of hair behind her ear for the seventh time and looks down at the printed Excel document.

Chapter 1

She shakes her head in honest confusion before pushing her thin wire frames up her nose and running an index finger across the paper before confirming, yet again, what she's just told me. Her face blooms a dark pink. "It must have been an oversight."

I sigh harshly but internally wince as the girl's face tightens. I know it isn't her fault per se, but the chief in me can't help but hold her to some level of accountability, considering she helps organize the event. "Quite the oversight, Lauren."

"I think it must have been the use of the word 'hot' in his submission. You didn't put that in yours, and that's probably why the system didn't pick it up as a duplicate entry."

I think my groan is inward until Lauren shifts uncomfortably, checking over her shoulder as if looking for help.

"How can a funnel cake be anything other than hot?" I knead my eyelids, trying my best to rein in the obvious agitation in my voice.

I don't mean to be an ass, but my tolerance for mistakes caused by disorganization, or someone relying on technology as if it's infallible, has my patience wearing incredibly thin. In my line of work, those sorts of slipups can cost someone their life.

"Perhaps we shouldn't get so upset at such a small mistake." The deep baritone in the voice behind me sears every nerve I have in unison. I grind my teeth together, preparing for an argument, but my opponent decides to add a little gas to my already smoldering fire. "I'm sure we can figure something out."

Figure something out.

Figure. Something. Out.

For nearly a decade, I've worked my ass off for my current position. Straight out of college, I came back to my sleepy hometown and took a position as a law enforcement officer. I worked under my father for years before he was forced to retire due to double knee replacements, and then the mayor appointed me as the chief of police over the department. It sounds like a huge accomplishment at my age, and while it partially is, in a city with a population of only about twenty thousand people, and a generation of Castillos being in the same position, it wasn't much of a decision on the mayor's part.

Especially since there was no one else who wanted it.

I mean, for one, it's not very exciting. The extent of my job rarely goes beyond making sure the local kids don't get too high and burn down the Jenkins' wheat farm, or helping Mrs. Jackson with the daily cat-in-a-tree catastrophes. The latter is technically a job for the firefighters, but I like Mrs. Jackson. Not to mention it's hard to resist the Irish coffee she makes me while dishing out some town gossip.

Honestly, though, I'm sure it also made it easier for the mayor to have someone that already knows the budget, or lack thereof, which brings me back to the problem at hand.

Because of the small funds allotted, the city throws a Fourth of July carnival every year where local entities such as the police, fire department, as well as the different art departments at the high school host fundraising booths. The funds earned have helped us immensely during the year and without their success, we wouldn't be able to afford some of the "noncritical" upgrades.

Last year, my officers and I had a funnel cake stand that did incredibly well. So amazing, in fact, that when the forms for our booth selections were emailed in May, it was a no-brainer. Since I didn't receive word that there was anyone else who chose the same fundraiser, I went and got all the necessary supplies. Some of my deputies even had their kids paint signs.

Imagine my surprise when the day of the carnival comes around and I'm blindsided to learn that my booth is next to the fire department's, which just so happens to be selling the same. Fucking. Thing.

Chapter 1

So, while I'd love to *figure something out*, I'm afraid that time has come and gone.

On better judgment, I decide to ignore the asshat behind me and force my attention back to Lauren. She's young, only having worked for the mayor a few years, but since she herself was once a participant in the carnival when she was in high school, she knows how important it is not to have active competition.

"How about we look and see who submitted their proposal first?" I ask, knowing it won't matter. It's too late for either of us to switch, but now, it's just to prove a point to the fire captain.

I hold my breath as Lauren's nervous gaze falls back to the paper, and at the same time, a tingle radiates down my spine. A telling sign his stare is locked on my back. I readjust my belt before letting my hand fall to the small pepper spray at my hip. I haven't ever had to use it, aside from that one occasion when a rat with rabies decided I needed to be his next meal, but I may have thrown it at the captain once. Or perhaps twice when he's pissed me off enough.

He grunts in response, his amusement evident, which only irritates me more.

Lauren sees something that makes her turn an even darker shade, but after running a hand through her blonde strands, she's able to steady her voice. "I didn't organize it by time submission when I exported the Excel sheet. So, I only have the date, and both of you filled out the form on May fifth."

"Can it be looked up on the computer?"

She winces. "I deleted the file after everyone filled it out."

"Of course you did." Resignation and annoyance work hand in hand as they force me to finally turn around.

Goddamnit.

Captain Ford stands relaxed a few feet behind me, a smug smirk pulling up one side of his stupidly perfect lips. His black tactical pants and fitted uniform shirt with the fire station insignia leave nothing to the imagination. The fabric is tight across his broad chest, the seams at his arms appearing to be made from magic thread as they stay intact through the constant strain. He lifts a brow, which is naturally arched—another thing I can't stand about men. Can someone explain why they always seem to have perfectly manicured eyebrows, thick lashes, and lush hair from using a two-in-one shampoo?

Like myself, he got his position when he was young, a generational advantage over the nonexistent competition. We were raised only a few houses down from one another, and our parents were constantly visiting each other. Both sides were always big on sharing stories and comparing their jobs, as well as the accomplishments of us kids.

I don't think it was ever in bad taste, but it created a competition between him and me, and soon, everything we did was to spite each other.

If he ran six laps during PE, I had to run seven. If I got a ninety on a math test, he had to get a ninety-one. If I dated the quarterback of the football team, he had to date the head cheerleader. This went on for years, and there was no corner of our lives that the rules of our competition didn't touch. So, when we ended up at the same college, I wasn't surprised.

Luckily, the police academy and the firefighter training program don't occupy the same space, or else it would have been chaos. I can almost picture it now—pranks, ruined clothes, missing shoes.

All of those examples fuel the logic behind me *knowing* that he did this on purpose.

Both our departments get together quite often for drinks and good conversation. Since our ongoing rivalry isn't a secret, it comes as no surprise that one night, a short time after last year's carnival, I got a little carried away, telling everyone about

Chapter 1

how the firefighters didn't make half of what my officers did. So, it only makes sense that he would figure out a way to finagle doing the same damn fundraiser.

It takes the full extent of my self-restraint not to say anything and merely walk past him.

Naturally, he doesn't let me get two feet before he ruins my relatively peaceful exit. "If you can't handle the heat of competition, you know you can just stay out—"

"I'd advise you to choose those next few words wisely, Kameron. Because last time I checked, you gave your latest girlfriend food poisoning. So I'd say it's you who needs to stay out of the damn kitchen." I continue on, relishing in his annoyed scoff as I all but stomp away from the assignment table like a toddler having a tantrum.

But as always, he has to have the last word. "Is that right? I mean, it was your mother's recipe, so…"

This forces my feet to a stop, and when I spin on my heels, I'm only half-surprised to see him a mere yard away. A stupid smirk is etched on his face as if it's permanent.

I narrow my eyes. "Bullshit."

He shakes his head, his dirty—no, *muddy*—blond strands falling over his forehead as he lifts two fingers. "Scout's honor."

Something between a strained laugh and scoff tumbles past my lips. His audacity is at an all-time high today, and it's clear he's trying to shake me up. Perhaps this is part of his plan to throw me off and win this game of ours. Too bad I intend to call his bluff.

"My mom would never trust you with—"

"Her trick for making her blueberry scones super thick and buttery is to freeze the—"

I nearly tackle Kameron as I slap a hand down shamelessly over his mouth. My own lips are parted in shock as I spear him with a menacing glare, both daring and threatening him to utter another word.

I can feel his smile stretch wider, his lids lowering in premature, victory smugness.

But being this close, with my chest nearly touching his, and the vibrant hues of his irises so clear I can make out three shades of blue, there's something else lingering in them. Something much more dangerous than his usual challenge.

The look makes my breath catch in my throat, and I tell myself it's from the shock of my mother's recipe betrayal that has my heart suddenly hammering into my rib cage. It has *nothing* to do with the heat from his body enveloping mine, despite the already warm air. It's *definitely* not his comforting amber scent or the way his gaze is dragging down my face, as if this is exactly what he intended.

"Asshole." My voice is nothing more than a heady whisper as I yank myself away from him and rub my offending hand on the hip of my shorts.

Kameron's smile stays intact, along with the fire burning brighter in the corner of his eyes. "Perhaps I'll make you a batch sometime, Aria."

I smirk, trying my best to keep an air of being unbothered, because I *am* unbothered. "The day I put anything of yours in my mouth will be the day I swallow fire."

This makes him chuckle. It's throaty and deep and I utterly loathe the way it always makes my stomach do a weird type of flip. Probably because I usually hear it after he wins at something and I want to sock him in the jaw.

"How about a wager, then?"

I lift a brow, my hand finding my hip. "I'm all ears."

He takes a step forward, and though I know I should move back, I don't allow him to win our standoff and straighten my

Chapter 1

spine instead. He stands only a foot away now, our chests almost reunited, forcing me to glance up to meet his eyes.

"If the firefighters make more money in tonight's booth, I get to put something of mine in your mouth."

I guffaw at his innuendo, ignoring the way it makes my stomach clench. I tilt my head to the side. "And *when* I win?"

Kameron shrugs. "Whatever your little heart desires."

My favorite part about our bets is when he finds himself being extra cocky and allows for open-ended bets. Nine times out of ten, those are the ones he wins, but when he doesn't, the payoff is all the sweeter.

"What do you say, Firefly?"

He moves just enough to hold a hand between us. I don't hesitate to grab it, and do what I've always done, and shake.

"Deal."

Aria
CHAPTER TWO

Am I currently stomping across the carnival grounds back toward my booth, feeling completely discombobulated? Maybe a little. But it's hard not to any time Kameron and I go head-to-head and he pulls *that* card.

The one where my skin feels like it's way too damn hot and my heart can't catch a steady rhythm.

I'm not blind, nor immune, to all that is Fire Chief Kameron Ford. He's a delicious six-foot-two, with insanely perfect jaw structure, and these cute freckles that span over the bridge of his nose. Let's not forget the dimple. The one on his left cheek, next to where his smile lines are.

He gets a few points deducted for the cliché blond hair and blue eyes, but at the same time, they give him an innocent type of look that contrasts against his dirty mouth.

And it's that mouth of his that makes my knees get a little less sturdy and has my pussy clenching around nothing. Kameron knows it too, which is why he uses it whenever I'm winning.

He doesn't fight fair, never has, and as a result, I end up back to the emotion men give me more often than not —annoyed.

Chapter 2

Well, there's that and frustration. Maybe it's those reasons alone why the vein in my neck is throbbing and sweat is beading at my temple, even though it's a gorgeous seventy degrees Fahrenheit.

"What'd he do?" My deputy and best friend, Elise, leans against our booth, a knowing smile on her face.

One of her long fingers is hovering over her phone midswipe, while the other musses with a loose brown tendril that's fallen from her bun.

I start to ask her how she knows, but remember it's not rocket science. No one gets under my skin like Kam.

With a heavy huff and an angry glance over my shoulder, I tell her the bad news. She stares at me wide eyed for a minute, a real "are you fucking kidding me" look pulling down her dark brows.

But then another beat passes and she shrugs, shoving her phone into her front pocket, and bending to grab a crate of supplies. "Are we really surprised, though?"

"No." I blow out another gust of air. "But that's pretty low, don't you think?"

Elise laughs, though there isn't much humor behind it. "He's gone lower before, hasn't he?"

I groan, the memory to which she's referring to instantly flashing through my mind. It was around the time our competitive nature took a turn toward a more sexual passive aggression.

It was the last day of our senior year, and we all skipped for ditch day. Half the class was out at the Jenkins' field, and to say we were all having a good time would have been an understatement.

My at-the-time crush and I snuck off, disappearing into the tall cornstalks. One thing led to the other, and soon I was topless and straddled over him.

That's when Kam found us.

He "accidentally" spilled an entire thirty-two-ounce fountain drink all over me as he tried to excuse himself.

The MVP of the basketball team shoved me off of him so hard that when my ass hit the ground, a loud thud accompanied my hiss of pain. It shot up my spine like lightning, and I mentally made a note to kick the guy when I stood up.

He tried to mumble an apology about just trying to shield himself from the cold ice, but I didn't catch the end because Kameron punched him in the face.

What happened after was a blur of screams, fists, and me yelling at them about how men as a whole are complete Neanderthals.

But then Kameron grabbed me, ignoring the hushed curses of my retreating now ex-crush, and pulled me to his chest.

It was somewhere between the heavy breathing, heated glares, and the way his eyes searched my face before they landed on my lips that everything changed. There was so much need in his eyes, and in the heavy rise and fall of his chest. I didn't know how I was going to react, but I did know I *wanted* the kiss he was about to give me.

But then he didn't. Instead, he gathered what little sense there was between us and moved backward.

He shook his head and said something about how he had made a mistake. How I was better off and safer with the likes of basketball players. Slightly confused and offended, I shoved him—albeit not very far—and asked what the hell that was supposed to mean.

It's not like I actively wanted him, not until that moment at least, and I couldn't understand why he wasn't giving in to the palpable energy pulsing between us.

But then he snatched me by the wrist and drew me close again. "Nothing about this is smart or safe, and it wouldn't end how you expect."

Chapter 2

A deep crease formed between my brow, the confusion from before becoming stronger.

Kam smirked, that dimple drawing my attention momentarily, before he chuckled. "You wouldn't behave, Aria. You'd come before I told you, and that would ruin all the fun."

The air thinned. It wasn't just his unspoken promise that drove my libido into overdrive, but the fact he spoke with such confidence. Like he knew what he was saying was an indisputable truth. But true to my nature, I didn't let it show how much his words affected me. I think I even had a good remark to spit back, but he didn't give me the chance.

He left before I could string the words together to form a sentence, and it was only when the heat of his body was gone and my skin prickled with goose bumps that I realized I was still half-naked.

The entire event changed the course of our rivalry. It became a game of wills that has gone on for more than a decade with no end in sight. I'd be lying if I didn't say it drives me insane.

Imagining him and me in bed, arguing with our bodies, committing to push one another in every way possible... it's hard not to want that. Even harder not to wonder.

To wish.

But then he pulls moves like he did today and I know for sure I'd likely strangle him rather than fuck him.

"Let's just focus on our booth, chief. I'm more than confident we'll reel in enough money to start those classes."

Elise's calm tone and attempt at redirecting my focus are appreciated. I nod, moving to help load the basket of whipped cream onto the table, and consider her words.

We don't get many calls for domestic violence or unprovoked attacks in our small town, but because of our size, we don't have a university. This forces kids who want to attend one to go to bigger cities. Too many times I've heard the stories and concerns of our community, worried about their children being in situations where a simple key chain pepper spray wouldn't protect them.

For a while, I wasn't too sure what I could do to help. Our kids went to college everywhere, some just a town over, others across the nation. But then one night, Elise and I were watching Margot Robbie kick ass in her female-led action movie and an epiphany hit.

People put in extreme situations with no prior training will be overrun with adrenaline and will either fight or take flight. Depending on the situation, one might be better than the other, though most citizens don't inherently know this. But the thing is, they can be taught.

That's when I decided what I'd be raising money for at this year's carnival. I want to hire certified trainers to come in and teach self-defense and preparedness classes to women.

I'll hold a special course for students that would include mediations, kickboxing, avoidance techniques, and basic defense skills. We already found the space—donated by an art teacher who no longer uses it—as well as all the trainers.

Nearly all the instructors are locals and have volunteered their time to teach the once-a-week class. But for the other teachers and protection equipment, we need to come up with the funds.

And we *will* come up with the funds. We have to.

Not only because of my competition with Kam, but the very real effect these classes will have, both on easing parents' fears when sending their daughters out into the world and the girls themselves. Primarily due to their increased confidence, knowing they're able to defend themselves.

With the vision in the forefront of my mind, my chest

Chapter 2

swells, renewed pride forcing my irritation from moments ago to ebb.

Between Elise and me, our booth is up and ready before my volunteer cops arrive. They set up the signs and got started prepping the plates and napkins. So far, I've done well to ignore the music and laughter of the firefighters just a few yards away, but now, as work begins to dwindle, I can't stop the heavy pull and let my eyes flash over to their booth.

Kam's back is to me as he lifts a box up onto the table. His muscles flex and ripple through the fabric of his shirt. He turns slightly, displaying the side of his face, and a heaviness moves into my stomach as I watch a lone drop of sweat tumble down his temple.

"Close your mouth before a bug flies in it and help me with this batter."

Elise nudges me on the shoulder at the same moment Kam locks eyes with me. His gaze drops down my frame, but before he can look back up, I turn around and give him a view of my ass—which looks phenomenal in my shorts, might I add.

I hear him give a glorified scoff, and I smirk to myself. I can guarantee heated gazes are just the appetizer of what he has planned to distract me, but he knows all too well that two can play that game, and I'm ready.

I fully intend on winning tonight, and I know exactly what I'm getting when I do.

Kameron

CHAPTER THREE

Contrary to what Aria thinks, I'm not a *complete* asshole.

In my defense, I didn't expect her to host a funnel cake stand two years in a row, and I *do* feel kinda bad about us having to compete for sales tonight. But also, if I'm being completely transparent, I'm thrilled at where the circumstances have brought us.

To this bet. This potential outcome. To the possibility of finally getting what I've been dying for since senior year. Hell, just the mere thought of it has my entire cardiovascular system throbbing, and it's that reason alone why I intend to win.

Maybe then I can find some damn peace.

See, Aria Castillo has always reminded me of English Ivy. At first glance, the plant is nothing more than any other green foliage. When it's still small, it's not really a big deal or something that even stands out among a bush of roses.

But then it starts to grow. Its tendrils stretch upward, wrapping around anything it can grasp, and soon, it's overtaking an entire wall, forcing its presence to be recognized. It's then you see it for what it really is.

It's beautiful. Breathtaking. Commanding and resilient.

Chapter 3

Overwhelmed by its sudden and extraordinary presence, it's easy to want to rip it out by the roots, tearing it from its place, and hope it will go away. But then it doesn't. It grows back, only this time somehow stronger and taller, and threatens to consume *everything*.

A lot of time has passed since I discovered the ivy affixed to my walls, and no matter how much I wonder what it'd be like to allow it free rein over the space, I know better. Being able to do that would mean cutting away vines and stripping leaves to mold it to what I want. And doing so would mean taking away from the magnificence of its innate wildness.

I know I can't, nor do I *want* to do that. But to let Aria thrive in my life would mean letting her utterly devour me, and in turn, completely suffocate me.

Which is exactly why I need to purge her from my system and get this infatuation—this desire—for her out of my head.

Like now. It's nearly impossible to look away from her.

Aria's dark-brown waves are pulled back away from her face in a loose ponytail, exposing a neck I want nothing more than to explore with my mouth. She locks her russet-tinted eyes on me briefly before spinning on her heels and strutting back to her booth. I know what she's doing, and I don't intend to fall victim like I have in the past.

Matter of fact, I'm still pissed off about a pool game she won a few months ago. She claims I'm the only one who plays dirty, but I think narrowly grazing a perfect ass like hers against my thigh is pretty shady as well.

"What's up with the chief?" one of my firemen, James, asks as I kneel to grab the last of the whipped cream canisters.

"She's pissed about us both doing funnel cakes." I shrug. "I didn't realize she was doing it twice in a row. There used to be a rule about not being able to do that, but I guess they changed it."

He pushes his dark hair from his face and frowns, glancing over at the officers' booth. I'd told him about it when I first got the call from the secretary. I guess he'd hoped I'd get them to back down and choose something else. "Yeah. Kinda sucks, though. We were banking on tonight to get the living quarters redone."

"And we still will. Aria is all bark and no bite—"

James nearly chokes on his laughter. "My ass. Name a time she hasn't been *all bite* and no bark. I'll wait."

I roll my eyes and fight the urge to look over at her again. "We're going to get the money for your damn sixty-inch TV and the foam toppers."

"Don't forget the room dividers for our beds," my other guy, William, pipes up from behind the large bowl of batter he's stirring. "If I have to look over at James with his hands down his pants one more time—"

"Yeah, yeah. It's on the list." I hold up a hand, not wanting to relive the moment Will saw James moisturizing his dick.

James shrugs, unfazed at the mention of his exhibitionism. "Whatever you say, cap. But with how serious the cops look over there, I'd say they came to play. I wonder what their fundraiser is."

I put on my gloves and lift one shoulder. As per the rules, no groups are allowed to disclose what their booths are raising money for. It prohibits guests from favoring one table all night, which in turn gives everyone the opportunity to rake in sales. But knowing Aria, it's probably for some more upgrades, more than likely of the technology variety.

Even though our town doesn't get a lot of calls in either of our departments, we like to stay ready in case we do. Not to mention our nearest neighboring cities are over double and triple our size, and if they ever call for help, we want to be able to do so adequately.

Chapter 3

"No telling. But our focus tonight is on winning."

William hands me a spoon, one of his bushy brows raised. "Win? You and Chief Castillo made a bet?"

I start to open my mouth, but James interjects. "Of course they did. These two can't go more than three days, tops, without betting on something."

"What are you going to win?" William asks.

Her.

Even though it was just a thought, I still bite down on my tongue hard enough to draw blood. I remind myself it's not her I'm winning, but the release of her from my mind.

But the momentary pause is enough for my men to pick up on something. They both have smirks on their faces as they wait patiently for me to speak.

My brows draw together as I put all my focus on filling the squeeze bottles with batter. "Nothing major. She's just going to eat one of our funnel cakes."

From my periphery, I see both of them jolt back comically in unison. Out of all the childish and almost silly things we make the other do when we win, this one is by far the most anticlimactic.

We've made the other eat or drink a lot of things in our lifetime, but never something normal. So plain.

"You remember the time she made you eat a lime that fell on the bar floor?" William makes a retching noise that's a little too wet.

"No, but then he got her back and had her take a shot out of Jordan's belly button," James adds, and we all burst into a fit of laughter.

Ninety percent of my guys are volunteers, and Jordan is one of them. His regular job is working the one farm we have, and his specialty is growing onions in only the best compost and manure. The man smells like he crawled from the deepest

Kameron

level in hell where the rest of the underworld's shit goes to fester.

Nice guy though, and the funniest one we know. Which is exactly why he was game when I suggested Aria take a shot out of his belly button.

In retrospect, I hadn't realized the man had washboard abs that she would take full advantage of. She ran her hands over his stomach so slowly he shivered and let a low sound come out of his throat that had me ready to call off the whole thing. But somehow, even with her staring at me through those thick eyelashes of hers, I was able to hold her gaze as she sucked every last drop of liquor from his belly button.

It was the first time I ever considered stroking my dick to Aria. It was so fucking hard, it hurt to walk, and all I could think about was having her mouth on me. Her hair wild, and her wrists cuffed. Cutting off every sense she has except taste...

It was difficult, but I was able to refrain like I have been my entire life because giving in would only make my curiosity about her grow. I'd want to know if she'd scream the way I imagine or if she'd squirm how I picture. If she'd be able to handle the heat of a flame as it flickers inches away from her spine.

I shake my head and return my attention to the conversation where they have recounted more bet outcomes. Not all of them are as extreme as dirty limes and smelly body crevices, but none of them are as simple as eating a funnel cake.

"So why?" William asks. "Seems a little boring."

"It's more of a prideful thing. I want her to know my funnels sold better *and* taste better than hers. And she'll have to taste that victory tonight."

Though it seems as if they have more to say on the matter, they both nod and return to the duties of setting up the booth.

There are only four full-time firefighters, but with one at

Chapter 3

the station manning the phones for any possible dispatches, it leaves only us three to run the fundraiser. Not a huge deal, but with neighboring towns coming by, I'm slightly worried we won't be able to keep up with the demand, forcing some to go next door to Aria's.

Still, we have toppings she doesn't and I have a trick up my sleeve just in case our line does dwindle smaller than hers.

Either way, I'm winning, and tonight, Aria will belong to me.

Aria
CHAPTER FOUR

"It's quiet, chief. Like always."

I nod into the phone, doing my best to ignore the heat on the side of my face. I'm certain it's from Kam trying to get me locked in one of our staring contests, but he's distracted me enough for the day.

"What about Mrs. Jackson?" I ask, propping my hip into the wood stand of our booth. All around me, people are adding the finishing touches to their stands while taking pictures to post on their social media. I make a mental note to have Elise do the same.

"I already checked on her. She's getting ready for the carnival just like the rest of the town, so no need to worry." My dispatch officer yawns before the faint but distinct sounds of a *Vampire Diaries* episode can be heard in the background. "But I'll walkie in if anything changes."

I let out a sigh. "Alright. Thank you. I'll be by later."

"Or you could tag along with Elise and go to the Red Velvet Bar tonight to let loose."

As if she heard her name, Elise glances at me from behind the containers of powdered sugar. One side of her lips hitches up and she nods while mouthing an elaborate *hell yes*.

Chapter 4

"Call me if anything happens," I repeat before hanging up and slipping my phone into my pocket.

"Why are you adamant about not coming out tonight? Have you ever heard the saying, 'all work and no play makes the chief a dull girl?'"

I purse my lips. "I'm pretty sure that's not how the saying goes. Also, it's the Fourth of July. Anything could happen."

Elise narrows me with a heavy gaze that tells me she can see right through my bullshit. "The only action that may happen will be within the acres of this carnival. Is this about the captain ogling you over there?"

As soon as I turn my head to look, I know I've given myself away and sigh.

She huffs out a humorless laugh. "You've never had a problem with him before. What's the issue now?"

"For one, his arrogance is on steroids." I hold up a finger.

"Nothing new. And you always up yours to match him."

Another finger. "Him cheating more often than not."

"How so?"

A quick glance over at my other deputies says they're too far gone in their own conversation to worry about mine. "He's pulling out the sex card too much now. It's frustrating. And distracting."

She lifts an arched brow. As someone I've known almost as long as I've known Kameron, it's not something she hasn't heard before. I mean, she was even there when I had a sickening little pity party after being abandoned horny in a cornfield. But the fact it's ever bothered me since then is new.

"You still wanna bang him?"

I push out a breath. "Is it completely pathetic if I say yes? But not in a true 'I'm attracted to you' way. More like a..."

I play with the words for a second and when I can't find the perfect ones, Elise does. "Like an 'I want to show you what you missed out on, and I could fuck circles around you' way?"

"Precisely."

As much as I'd love to deny it, I *am* bothered that he's able to walk around with the ability to say he turned me down. And even more so because he probably believes the bullshit he spewed out of his mouth about me not being able to hold an orgasm.

Ha. That in itself is laughable. I've never met a man who made me come during sex. Not one. And in my experience, the prettier the guy is, the lazier he is in bed. So I can almost bet my bottom dollar he'd end up being a missionary warrior with a ten-pump maximum.

And I so want to have that ammo in my arsenal.

Yes, I'm aware of how it sounds, and I know I'm probably taking the whole competition a little far, but also, why not? Life's too short to not win a sex competition.

"What are you smirking at?" Elise moves around the table and hands me a pair of gloves.

I shake my head and put them on, tampering down the sudden influx of butterflies in my stomach. "How I'm going to win this and then sit on his face and see if that will shut him up."

She laughs and juts her head in the direction of the firefighters. "I bet he'd find a way to talk shit while also tongue fucking you."

"Maybe. But then I'd sit all the way down."

"You'd suffocate him?"

A wide smile stretches across my face. "Isn't that how every man wants to go? Death by pussy?"

We both break into a fit of giggles, garnering the attention of everyone within earshot, but it doesn't deter us. If anything,

Chapter 4

it makes us laugh harder as we turn on the generator and get ready for the first wave of guests appearing at the entry gate.

I'd be lying if I said I wasn't at least a little nervous about the evening. Yes, it would suck to lose to Kameron and have to deal with his arrogant-ass victory lap. But most importantly, I'm worried about letting down the dozens of girls who just graduated and are going off to college this fall.

The mayor has strict policies in place about crowd fundraising after the carnival. He doesn't want the town to feel obligated or guilt ridden, hence the festival in the first place. This means if it doesn't happen this year, we have to wait for next summer, which could potentially put one of them in a situation I could have prepared them for but didn't.

A new ripple of frustration moves through me, clouding my calm mind. Against my better judgment, I give in to the constant pull of Kameron's presence and grant him a last second glare. It's one I imagine two racers give each other before the red light flips to yellow and then green, releasing angry drivers onto the NASCAR track.

His blue eyes collide with mine, and in them is the same challenge. The same dare. We both want the same exact thing, and we both want to be the first to get it.

The butterflies from earlier whip into a frenzy so fast I can almost swear I feel the edges of their wings slicing into my stomach.

You've got this. Take a breath.

I do. I take about seven. It's not enough to quell the anxiousness of tonight, but it does the job of soothing the raging butterflies.

As if on cue, Lauren, now dressed in a fun and flirty little red number, walks onto the magician's stage set up in a central location. She taps the mic twice to get all of the vendors' attention.

Aria

"As always, we'd like to thank everyone for coming out and participating in this year's carnival. Although we may have had a hiccup here and there"—her gaze flashes in Kam and I's direction briefly before she continues—"I truly think tonight will be one of Liberty Fall's best! Have fun, make money, and we hope you stick around for the fireworks after!"

A small round of applause and cheers run through the crowd but quickly dies down as they open the front gate and the public begins pouring inside.

At first, I assume most everyone will go to the bright lights of the rides and carnival games, like they do every year. But the local reading circle stops in front of my stand, and all order my first funnels of the night.

I start to shoot a smirk in Kam's direction but see he's already making his own cakes for some bikers.

Shit. There are at least a dozen more of them.

"Can I have some extra powdered sugar, darling?" one of the ladies asks, and I'm grateful for the refocus.

I nod a quick yes and get to work.

Despite my earlier trepidation, thirty minutes pass, and the sweat rolling down my spine is proof enough that we'll make our goal in no time. Excitement swells in my chest as the girls and I work to keep up with the consistent orders, and soon, Kam and our bet are far from my mind.

I'm winning. It's not even a question anymore. He probably knows it too.

And it's right as I think it that I remember how sore of a loser he is. How when he feels like he's about to lose, it's then he cheats.

I know it before I even look over, but it pisses me off nonetheless to see it.

That fucking asshole.

Aria
CHAPTER FIVE

Drowning in my own funnel cake orders, I haven't bothered to peer over at Kameron's line since we got our first customers. In a way, it was a strategic move, so I didn't psych myself out if his line got longer than mine. But knowing he'd cheat, I had to make sure.

And of course, I was right.

His line is long. So long, it has to curve and wraps around the side of a few booths. One might ask, why stand in a line when there are a bazillion different things to buy and a dozen rides to get on? Well, I'm confident the answer is because three firefighters wearing tac pants and skintight tank tops are making a show of serving funnel cakes.

And not just your run-of-the-mill funnel cakes. Nope. That would be too simple for the likes of Kameron Ford.

If the stacks of muscles flexing through the thin white material of their tanks weren't enough, they also are seductively dancing to an upbeat song I could almost swear I've heard on one of my niece's princess movies.

Oh, and let me not forget to mention they're pouring on hot fudge and whipped cream toppings like they're in an amateur porn flick. As a result of the way he's flinging it on, some of the

Aria

residual chocolate is painting Kam's ridiculously sculpted biceps.

Even annoyed, the sight makes the muscles in my lower abdomen uncomfortably tight, and it's clear that's the whole point.

The same book club ladies who were our first patrons are in their line now, giggling as they watch the men make a dessert they more than likely won't even eat. And they aren't the only ones. My eyes skim down the remaining people waiting and find at least half a dozen of them who've already ordered one from us.

It doesn't bother me in terms of meeting my goal, but it makes me realize winning the bet is now next to impossible.

A fresh round of irritation swells in my chest as I greet the next customer with a forced, thin-lipped grin. It's Mr. Thomas, the owner of a coffee shop I frequent nearly every day before work. He's a kind older gentleman who knows how to make an iced coffee to put Starbucks to shame. It doesn't surprise me when he decides not to comment on my perturbed expression and instead smiles politely as he tells me he needs two large cakes—one of which with no powdered sugar.

I nod and trade places with one of my deputies, Jim, before joining Elise on the other side of the fryers.

So far, our carousel way of taking orders has kept us moving both quickly and efficiently. We take an order, move to make it, rotate to plate it, slide over to finish it off with sugar, and shift one last time to hand it off.

"You good?" Elise nudges me lightly on the shoulder.

"I knew he would pull this crap, but still, it irks the hell out of me." I squeeze the batter into the hot grease, watching as the lazy swirls and circles come together.

Elise uses tongs to poke at her almost perfectly browned cake. "I get it. That's why we brought our own backup plan."

Chapter 5

Pushing out a big breath, I watch her take out an order and place it on the draining tray. She quietly waits for me to make the call—the decision—to stoop down to Kam's level. To balance the playing field even though it means I'd be a cheater just like him. There have been many times I've wanted to do it, only to prove a point, but decided to take the high road and lose. It let me keep my air of confidence, knowing he can never really beat me fair and square.

But tonight has me teetering on the edge, considering for once what it'd be like to give him a taste of his own damn medicine.

After Elise plates her funnel cake, she moves to the powdered sugar and sighs. I can see the disappointment curving the edge of her lips downward. "We don't have to. I've been keeping tabs. We'll make enough to cover our supplies, so it's not necessary to beat him. I just want you to win. That way, he can suffocate with your pussy, y'know?"

This coaxes a surprised laugh out of me as I take out my own order and drain it. "Yeah, I get it. Honestly, though, I'm kind of nervous if I did win. Like what if he was completely horrible at it?"

She calls out her customer's name before scoffing. "Then you'd have enough to keep his mouth shut till at least New Year's."

"Yeah, the only silver lining after being left with a blue vagina—"

"Blue vulva," she corrects.

I laugh again. "Yeah, as if that makes the term seem any better. But you get what I'm saying."

She nods, and when she opens her mouth to add something else, it's almost as if she thinks better of it and snaps it shut.

My brows squeeze together, but I don't get to ask her what she was going to say because she takes the next order while I call out to Mr. Thomas to pick up his. It isn't until we're next to each other again that she narrows me with a suddenly serious gaze.

The look alone is enough to make a knot form in my throat. Elise is rarely serious. "What?"

She bites on the side of her cheek, seemingly still deliberating if she's going to tell me what she's thinking. But after another moment, she relents. "Aria. What if he's good at it? Like, really good at it?"

The carnival is loud with excitement, laughter, and the giddy screams of those on the rides, but the loud cackle I let past my lips erupts into the energized air, attracting a few glances.

"I have a knack for this sort of thing, Elise. Otherwise, I wouldn't dare broach the subject. The day in the cornfield, he had an opportunity—a chance—to finish what me and the guy had started. I was topless, for fuck's sake. But did he take it? No. He gave me some bullshit spiel about how I was 'safer' with basketball players."

Elise considers my words as we move in tandem, working to get our orders done.

"He didn't miss the opportunity, and he didn't do it out of my *safety*. Kameron did it because he realized he was about to have to put his money where his mouth was and he knew he wouldn't be able to deliver."

My eyes flash to the man in question, who's moving around his booth with his firefighters like a well-oiled machine.

No matter what rivalry Kam and I have going on, watching him with his men is a work of art, and I don't just mean around a fryer.

We've only had a few fires since Kam and I came back to town, most small and not resulting in much damage. But we've

Chapter 5

been called out about a dozen times to nearby cities that weren't as fortunate.

The gut-wrenching feeling I get when watching them disappear in the middle of a blaze is something I can never truly describe. It's one of deep despair, helplessness, and overall fear that grips the entire body. It's in those moments when I'm helping secure the perimeter to civilians that I can never get enough air. The unknown is so exhilarating, it seizes my muscles and pushes every other sense I have into high alert.

I become overstimulated, oversensitive, and it isn't until I see Kam's outline emerge from the flames that I can fill my lungs again.

But I can't lie. Watching him work with them out there is incredible. It's a language that no one else knows how to speak. I can't deny that despite how much I want to punch him in the face for even the smallest infraction, I also want to rip his uniform off and fuck him right next to the inferno. (After everyone is out and safe, of course.)

Kameron must feel me staring because he glances up just as he's piling on an unnecessary amount of whipped cream on a funnel cake. His lips curl on one side, his smuggest of smirks on full display as he shoots me a wicked wink.

It's hard to ignore the clench and residual tingles the action leaves me with, but it also sparks a healthy dose of annoyance.

"It's time I show him what a cocky demeanor really is." I strip the gloves off my hands, flinging them in the trash bin. The new resolve washes over me as I slip out the back of our area and toss Elise a parting smirk, not too unlike the one Kam just gave me. "I'll distract the oaf. You get the box."

Elise nearly squeals before jumping to do as told. "Yes, chief."

Kameron
CHAPTER SIX

Here's the number one thing I will not miss after fucking Aria out of my system; the physical response I have to her presence.

It's been this way since we were kids and has only evolved over the years, somehow becoming increasingly more nerve racking. No matter how long has passed, every time I see her, my heart nearly doubles its pace. When she's close enough that I can smell the tropical fragrance of her shampoo, my chest squeezes. And when we touch, even with the slightest brush of hands, my nerves feel like they're on fire.

Every part of me aches to reach for her, and more often than not, I end up having to awkwardly readjust my hard-on. And when she opens that mouth of hers?

A tremor runs down my spine at the thought of taking her mouth—both with my own and with my cock.

The only thing I'm worried about is if by doing so, by finally giving in, we'll be opening Pandora's box. If one night, one time, isn't enough.

It has to be.

I give myself another reminder, the one I've had to tell myself over a dozen times and push out a heavy sigh.

Chapter 6

Fucking Aria and *fucking* her are two very different things. While I'm sure she wouldn't mind some of the things I'd like to do to her, I know others would be off the table.

See, Aria thrives on being in control. She needs to know everything about a situation so she can analyze the hell out of it before making a decision and delegating tasks. Being in charge means everyone is trusting her to make the right call. To not be overcome by emotion or slip up due to anxiety.

Being with me would mean taking a lot of that—if not all of it—away. It would mean trusting me when she can't see, when she can't hear, when she can't speak.

She would need to know that even though I would take away every sense she has, she would still *be* in control.

And that's not Aria.

Handcuffing her wouldn't make her feel liberated but trapped. Blindfolding her wouldn't make her more sensitive to my touch but overwhelmed. Filling her ears with *Handel* while teasing her with my tongue wouldn't drive her into delirium but probably stress her.

My little firefly isn't meant for me, which is why this needs to be one and done. Maybe we can prove to each other once and for all that we're best suited as competitive rivals and nothing more.

William yells out another order over the loud music, at the same time, the fine hairs on my neck rise. I don't have to turn around to know she's there, especially since my pulse has already begun thrumming.

I ignore her for a moment, squeezing the batter into the hot grease while bobbing my head casually to the tempo of "Feels Like the First Time." The pale swirls quickly begin to rise, connecting with one another as small bubbles fizz everywhere. I keep my gaze on the browning batter as I speak over my shoulder.

"Is there something I can help you with, chief?"

When she doesn't respond, I almost give in to the magnetic pull to look at her. But lucky for me, it's time to flip my funnel cake.

Momentarily occupied but never distracted from her presence, my body hums as she rounds the table and stands on the opposite side of the fryer. Her brown eyes scan my mess of a workstation before she murmurs something to herself about pretty men and glances up at me.

When our eyes connect, my dick and heart tic in tandem. She's so fucking gorgeous; it's difficult to look at her without smiling. Without wanting to *touch* her.

God, this woman is infectious.

Even surrounded by concert-level noise, the silence between us is heavy. She stretches it out until I no longer think the sweat beading on my temple is from the warm air or the heat rising from the oil but from her. From the way her gaze rakes over my body, taking in every muscle, every stain of chocolate, every jump of my vein.

When I shift to throw the funnel cake inside a Styrofoam container, she quietly watches me. Her demeanor is nothing if not merely observant, and I decide to make light in the dense air before I literally combust and throw her over my shoulder, bet be damned.

"Wow, chief. I know we got stuck with the same booth, but I didn't think you'd be so blatant in your attempt to copy what we're doing."

The slightest twitch of her lips is all I'm granted before she nods to my appearance. "I'm fairly certain if I were to duplicate what's getting you all these sales, I'd have to lock myself up for indecent exposure."

I let out a grunt of laughter. "Maybe. But I'd enjoy the show."

Chapter 6

"I'm sure you would, Captain Ford." She shifts her weight back on her heels before tucking both her hands in the back pockets of her shorts.

It was a move to get me to look at her thighs and I fall for it. The smooth, tan flesh is yet another perfect part of her that mocks me when I close my eyes.

Rather than give away the sudden heat rising up my back, I let my tongue peek out and run it along the edge of my bottom lip. I drag my gaze up her frame as slowly as possible until even the ice queen herself can't control the unsteady rise and fall of her chest nor the blush creeping up the column of her delicate neck.

When I reach her eyes, I'm greeted with fire. Her irises burn with the same need that's tangled in my chest, only there's a difference in hers.

Aria's is pure hunger. Her desire for me is a tension she wishes to break. A string so close to snapping she probably thinks that once it does, so will everything else between us.

Can't say how I feel is *too* much different, only for me, it's more out of hope that I can prove to myself we aren't a good fit. It will help rid myself of the fascination I have with her and I can move on to a more suitable match.

Hope being the key word.

William yells another few orders, prompting me to focus. I quickly sprinkle some powdered sugar on top before squirting a dollop of whipped cream. It isn't until I take the bottle out of the warmer to squeeze out the hot fudge that Aria moves.

Despite knowing it's hot, she tilts her index finger up, catching the first bit of fudge dripping from the tip of the bottle.

She sucks in a sharp breath as it touches her skin, but she doesn't budge until the entire edge of her finger is covered in chocolate. I feel like I'm stuck in a trance, watching her move in slow motion as she takes her finger back and slides it past her parted lips and into her mouth.

The air catches in my throat as she closes those lips around her finger and allows the smallest moan to escape her throat.

My nerves ignite, my blood surges, and it takes every ounce of self-control I have not to pluck that finger from her mouth and devour her whole.

Her eyelashes flutter open, revealing a gaze much heavier than before, and without another word, she brushes past me. When her shoulder briefly connects with mine, a tremor shakes down my limbs and a satisfied giggle floats in the air behind her.

The sound is triumphant but for once, I couldn't care less. Aria just opened a box neither of us had any clue she had the key to, and now I'm forced to rethink everything.

"Is this my order Captain Ford, or?" The question is from one of the elementary school teachers, who is looking anywhere but at me, her cheeks flushed a light pink.

I look down at the funnel cake still missing hot fudge. I nod, shoving the bottle Aria touched away and grabbing a new one, quickly finishing her order.

When the teacher leaves, I notice a large portion of our line has suddenly moved as well. Only, it isn't because they grew tired of waiting or decided to go hop on one of the festival rides. It's Aria's stand.

Everyone's crowding around, nearly toppling over the deputy trying to get everyone in an orderly line.

The notion she went and took her shirt off makes my hypothetical hackles rise and all at once, I don't care that William or James are calling after me.

Red encroaches my vision as I approach her booth and suddenly I'm reminded of the day in the cornfield. When I caught that ball player with his hands all over my firefly, I

Chapter 6

nearly lost it. Now, I'm fully prepared to spray any spectators away with my truck's hose.

Only, when I reach the front of her line, it isn't her without a shirt on. It's me.

Me and my entire crew of firefighters.

Aria
CHAPTER SEVEN

Though I'm not sure what Kam thought he was going to see when he started charging like a bull over to my side, I know it wasn't the long-lost calendars from last year.

I'm already back behind the stand, squeezing batter into the fryer when he emerges, wide eyed and fists balled at his sides. His eyes flash to me first, the momentary scan over my chest forcing me to bite into my lip to keep from laughing.

It's less interesting to me he thought I'd take my top off and more so his actual reaction to the possibility. A vein I rarely see is pulsing on the side of his neck, and his hair is even mussed like he ran a stressed hand through it. It's challenging to say the least, to ignore the visceral response my body has as he relaxes to seeing me fully clothed.

I shouldn't like seeing Kam's jealous side, but it's so rare and so damn delicious that I can't help but appreciate the sight.

There's also the small truth that it gives me a piece of my sanity back, knowing that somewhere deep down, he wants me just as much as I want him, and this isn't all just a game. In a way, it reinforces what I told Elise earlier about him being scared he wouldn't be able to deliver.

Chapter 7

A deep line appears between his eyebrows as they come together, confusion marring his expression until his gaze lands on the calendars.

Last year, the firefighters did a cliché half-naked shoot for a calendar, complete with the cutest damn puppies and kittens. The guys brought the sample they ordered when we met up for drinks one night and seeing Kam like that...

Long story short, the calendar was fucking hot. So hot, Captain Ford decided to do a less explicit version so it would sell more. Something about wanting more wives being comfortable hanging it around their husbands and whatnot.

We all tried to talk him out of it, but he's so damn hardheaded he already had the new photo shoot scheduled before we paid the tab later that night.

Being that they ordered the calendars from a small printing press, she couldn't get a lot done before the festival, so they sold out quickly. Hence why my department put them to shame in sales.

Anyway, fast forward a couple of months and I'd just lost a bet with Kam on how many shots he could take while still being able to get a perfect score on the basketball arcade game in the back of the bar. He'd won me as his designated driver for the next two months, and I was heated. One of those nights, I got roped into taking him and William back to the firehouse. I saw the box of old calendars they decided not to use and asked William if I could have them.

Half-drunk, and half-curious, he gave them to me with a knowing smirk. For the longest time, I didn't know what I was going to do with them but kept them around for a rainy day.

Well, consider it's pouring, because those bad boys are out on a table, and now free with every two funnel cakes ordered.

Kameron's face goes through at least five different emotions before he's able to piece everything together and land on something eerily close to impressed. His blue eyes light up at the corners and he nods slowly as he takes a step backward.

"Alright, Firefly. You want to play? Let's play."

With a parting smirk and butterflies waging a war in my stomach, he turns around, disappearing into the crowd.

The rest of the night, I'm on edge. Part of me is waiting for Kam and his boys to pull some kind of stunt, while the other part is trying frantically to keep up with orders and keep my mind focused.

Still, I feel a little dirty having cheated. The win—and I will win—won't feel as good, considering I had to drop down to Kam's level.

"Stop overthinking it. We almost tripled our freaking goal," Elise says, sorting the money into a little metal box as I clean up our mess with my other deputies.

I bite into the corner of my lip and stretch my neck from side to side. I mean, don't get me wrong, I'm happy—no, *grateful*—we made enough for the classes. Hell, I'm ecstatic I probably won the bet, but the satisfaction that comes with it while playing fair isn't here.

"How much were we at before the calendars?"

Elise rolls her eyes. "Chief, you won, it doesn't matter how. He does this kind of stuff all the time."

It hits me as the words come out. It's not that I had to pull out a trick to beat him, it was the *type* of trick I had to use. "I don't like the fact that I used *his* picture to get us there, though."

She sighs, snagging the receipt paper from her bag and unrolling it. "What time was it?"

"A few minutes after seven."

Her eyes look over the paper until she finds the total. "We were at nine hundred, give or take a few bucks."

I nod and glance over at Kam's booth. They're almost done

Chapter 7

breaking down their setup and it won't be long before he comes asking how much we made.

"You're not seriously going to go off that amount, are you?" Elise stands, her voice bordering on a plea. "Don't let him win. You deserve tonight, Aria."

Shaking my head, I slip my phone from my back pocket and call the station, still undecided. It only rings once before my dispatch officer picks up. "Hey, chief. All's good here."

"Not one call?"

The sound of a vampire tussle comes to a halt as she pauses her show. Papers ruffle in the background before she finds the pad of paper she uses to jot things down. "The light on Elm is acting funny. It only allows traffic through on the south for about ten seconds before it turns yellow. Reports of firecrackers on the outskirts of town, but a squad car said the kids were just waiting on the carnival's fireworks display to start and have since dispersed."

"That's it?" I inquire further, though I know it probably is.

"Yep. So go enjoy the fireworks show and please have fun with Elise tonight. We have plenty of people on patrol."

I sigh but relent, thanking her for her time before hanging up and tucking my phone back into my pocket.

Glancing down at my watch, I see there are about twenty minutes left until the rides close and about thirty left until the bonfire and firework display. Normally I don't stick around for the whole thing, but something in me doesn't feel like celebrating down at the Red Velvet. Something tells me the firefighters will probably claim the same thing I'm thinking and say that technically they *helped* me win the bet because I used their calendars.

I should have just worn a tank top.

A few minutes pass before we have our area broken down and cleaned up. I promise Elise I'll call her in a bit and head to the mayor's checkout table to sign the form. Naturally, Kam is already there—albeit now fully clothed—smiling at the mayor's secretary while making casual conversation.

From the looks of it, he's already done his checkout, so why he's still hanging around chatting it up with Lauren is beyond me. A spike of irritation flutters through me, but I tamp it down immediately.

Jealousy is best suited for chick flicks and romance books.

Ignoring him, I bend and sign the paper. Kam's gaze burns into the side of my face, but he continues the trivial conversation with Lauren. They are arguing about what's better on a funnel cake—something hot or something cold.

I set the pen down with a loud thud and look Kam directly in his eyes. The cool-blue color is darker than usual.

Unbothered and unasked, I drop my input. "Cold needs to be paired with hot. The contrast on the palate is both intense and satisfying."

Kam's eyes flare, but I don't wait to see another reaction and instead spin on my heels and walk to my squad car.

His heavy steps sound behind me, and the closer he gets, the faster my heart pumps. I tell myself I'm annoyed with the very real chance I'm going to lose the bet, and it has nothing to do with hearing his approach while not being able to see him.

It has nothing to do with the anticipation of when he'll be next to me. What he'll *do* or *say* when he's next to me.

Get a grip, horndog.

I internally scold myself just as I reach my car, parked only a few yards away from where our booth was. I reach for the door, but Kam's large hand makes an appearance, hitting the top of my car and caging me in on one side.

"Where you going, Firefly?"

I roll my eyes. "You and that nickname."

Having been in the Liberty Falls version of the Girl Scouts

Chapter 7

since I was in kindergarten, you'd think that's where I earned the name. But nope, according to him, that wasn't it at all.

I was sixteen when my family was over at Kam's during a block party. They had a firepit going in the back, and it drew me in almost immediately. The way the flames flickered and danced, releasing embers into the night air, was so enticing I was almost transfixed in my spot. I watched in a trance and moved as close as I could, reveling in the warmth that radiated from the small blaze.

It was Kam who yanked me away, fussing at me about trying to turn myself into a Rice Krispies Treat. Later, I asked him what he thought about me being a firefighter.

Still, to this day, I don't think I've ever heard him laugh as loud as he did that night. After I'd had enough and my annoyance meter was beyond capacity, I punched him in the gut.

He doubled over, half groaning, half still laughing, but he finally gave me an answer. He said, "You need to be able to put it out, Firefly, not chase it like a moth to a flame."

When I asked him about the name, he simply smirked and told me he'd tell me one day. I guess I've gotten so used to it that I forgot to ask.

I turn around and find myself face to face with Kam. His body envelops mine, the heat from him almost stifling as it invades my lungs, carrying with it his warm scent. His gaze is hooded, yet somehow playful, half-hidden under the locks of blond hair that have fallen over his forehead.

My core tightens, and my pulse thrums, both his proximity and appearance doing unnecessary things to my nether regions.

His lips tug up on one side as if he can sense the array of emotions working through me. "Yeah, still with the nickname."

"You never told me where you get it from." My voice is too breathy for my liking, but who can blame me?

"Maybe you can use a bet one day to find out."

I tilt my head, raising one annoyed brow. "You can't just tell me?"

"Where's the fun in that?"

"Just tell me," I sigh, jiggling the keys in my hand, making my soon-to-be exit known.

"How about you tell me how much you made off my chiseled chest."

I fucking knew it.

I yell an internal, "I told you so" at Elise before rolling my eyes. "Before I started giving away your calendars, we were at nine."

His brows tic together and his head jolts back slightly. "Before? You don't want to include after?"

I shake my head. "Nope. Because I really don't feel like hearing you run your mouth for a whole year about how *you* got me the win."

This makes Kam chuckle. It's low and breathy, and why my cunt can't behave for two freaking minutes is beyond me. "So you'd rather lose than include those sales?"

I nod. "Yep."

"You're so fucking stubborn. You know that?" He backs away, taking his overwhelming presence with him, and digs his phone from one of his dozens of pockets. He taps on the screen before holding it up to his ear.

What are you doing? I mouth.

He ignores my question and for a moment I think of socking him in the jaw, but then he speaks into the receiver. "Hey, Will. Can you look up how much we made around—"

Kam looks at me, and for a second, I can't believe what's happening. He lifts an impatient brow to which I answer, "Seven."

"Seven," he says.

Chapter 7

We both wait for what seems to be an eternity before he nods, muttering a quick *thanks*, and hangs up.

When he looks back at me, I could almost swear my heart is in my throat. Though I'm unsure if it's because Kam is playing fair for once in his life, or from trepidation while waiting to see who beat who.

He lets the anxiety hang before he glances off toward the carnival rides. "Here's what I'll do. Take a ride with me on the Ferris wheel, and I'll use the seven o'clock time to determine the winner."

"And if I don't?" I ask cautiously, watching for any tell of emotions on his face.

He turns back to me, a classic Kam smirk imprinted on his face. "Then you lose, Aria Castillo. And that mouth belongs to me."

Aria
CHAPTER EIGHT

We walk to the Ferris wheel in silence, and while I think I'm doing a good job of playing bored, inside, my mind is going a thousand miles a minute. At this point, I'm nothing more than jumbled nerves and a million questions.

For one, why does he want to ride the Ferris wheel? Moreover, why does he want to sit in a closed compartment a hundred feet off the ground? And a hundred feet might not even be doing the gigantic thing justice. A few years back, the mayor paid a pretty penny (though it actually came from the fees he charges us to host booths) to buy the massive wheel. It has around thirty cabins that are enclosed, which I appreciate because it lessens the fear factor of falling out. Not that I'm scared of heights or anything.

Maybe I am a little.

Oh, okay, that makes sense. It's not being with *him* that's got my pulse racing, it's from the heights.

A little more relaxed, I smile at the operator when we approach the ride.

He greets us both. "You'll be the last ones on. We're going

Chapter 8

to go around three times, then I'm going to start letting people off, and you'll be the last I unload. Is that okay?"

Before I can answer, Kam does. "Perfectly fine. Thank you, Jimmy."

Jimmy nods in response and moves ahead of me, opening the side for the both of us to climb in.

We sit on opposite sides and wait for him to secure us in with a click of the little door.

When the ride starts with a small jerk and we're lifted into the air, we remain as quiet as we were when walking the carnival grounds. I take the moment to breathe, choosing to focus on the sights surrounding us rather than the suffocating air between us.

It's clear he's playing one of his games, and instead of feeding into it, or the steady climb of the ride, I find the top of a ring toss game and focus on the old, weathered red fabric.

There are rips on the tops that have been either patched or sewn together like stitches. Half the triangular flags that hang from the sides have been lost to time, while the string holding its cone position is a good windstorm away from snapping off.

The momentary distraction helps me grab one of the dozens of questions floating around in my head, and it's only when we've completed our first loop around that I finally decide to just ask.

"Why are you going to use the seven o'clock time to determine who wins?"

His blue eyes flash to me before he slowly turns his face. "Why not?"

I scoff. "Because that's very unlike you, Kam. You do damn near anything to make sure you win."

He shrugs, seemingly entertained by my slight frustration at having to explain the obvious. "Perhaps I was a little impressed with that stunt you pulled. It was very *unlike* you."

"Yeah right, I'm not an idiot. You're going to *allow* me to win this when really you'll tell everyone you *let* me win."

"Or how about *I'm* not a complete asshole and play it fair? It's not like we won't have a new bet going on in two weeks."

He got me there. Whether it's a sport playing on the TV, or a quick game of quarters, we don't go long without making a spectacle of one another. Hell, I look forward to the shenanigans with Kam at the end of my workweek. They're damn near the highlights, if I'm being honest.

"Still," I mumble. "You're not one to just give a win, even if you're impressed. There was that time I hit your dart out of the board and got a bull's-eye, and you still called foul because my foot crossed over the line."

This makes him smile, and my stomach does a flip. I attribute it to swaying in the cab as we reach the peak of the ride.

"Aria, you win this one, okay? So tell me what you want."

"What I want?" I repeat his words. *What I want?*

Hell, six hours ago, I knew exactly what I wanted, but having to say it now, confined in this small space with no spectators to spur us on, feels foreign. But if I don't, I think I'll die from the nagging Elise will put me through. Or at least want to pluck my ears from my head.

"Aria."

Kam's low baritone snaps me back to him. He's leaning forward, both forearms propped against his knees. My fingers itch to brush the hair still draped across his forehead.

My nerves sing as I open my mouth to push out the words, but as if the world is giving me a warning, the cab stops just as it reaches the bottom. Jimmy calls out that this is our last go-round before he's going to start letting us off, which should take about fifteen minutes.

Chapter 8

It isn't until we start to rise again that I look back at Kameron.

He's got the cocky smirk on his face, the one I usually want to slap off. "My men seem to think you're all bite and no bark. But they don't know you like I do, Firefly."

The condescending undertones in his words don't go unnoticed, and I find myself back in my comfortable state of perpetual annoyance. "They don't, just like they don't know their fearless leader is nothing more than a slimy cheater that wouldn't have won half our bets if he played them straight."

Kam guffaws. "There are no rules in our petty games, Aria. And stop trying to act all high and mighty, like you don't shove your ass in my direction every chance you get in hopes of distracting me."

"It's not my fault you're distracted by my ass."

His humorless laugh in response is loud. "Spare me. All you are is one huge distraction."

I jolt back, my blood pressure climbing with every passing second. "What the hell is that supposed to mean?"

"Did you know firefly larvae glow to warn predators that their blood is toxic? But when they get older, it's to attract a mate?"

This halts the insult I had ready to hurl and instead confusion mixes in. "What does that have to do with anything, Kameron?"

He shakes his head. "Doesn't matter. Now, tell me what you want."

What I want is to slap him into next week, then go home and relieve some of the tension he's caused me. But instead, I push out a breath and meet his serious gaze with my own.

I'm not a shy person, and when it comes to getting what I want, especially in bed, I'm even less so because I always have to do work if I want to finish. But the way his eyes are shifting into something darker—something so unlike him—the more the words get caught in my throat.

The ride is on its way down and if I don't say it now, I probably won't.

Just say it, Aria.

I briefly close my eyes, channeling my inner sex goddess out of her chrysalis, and when my eyelashes flutter open, she's in full control.

A challenge filters into my voice. "I want you to make me come before we get off this ride."

Kameron's pupils flare and a nerve in his jaw tics. But it's a brisk show of emotion that passes as quickly as it came.

He tilts his head to the side slightly. "How?"

I shrug, ignoring the heaviness that's settled low in my stomach. "However you see fit."

"And if I succeed?"

"This isn't a new bet, Kam. This is my reward for winning at the booth."

He smirks, and the moment the ride stops for the cab to empty behind us, he moves to sit next to me.

The heat I felt as he hovered over me at my car pales in comparison to the blaze radiating off him now. The air suddenly seems a little too thin while my heart hammers against my rib cage so loud, I think he might hear it.

If he notices, he doesn't say because his right arm curls around my waist and digs into my upper thigh. The sensation of his tight grip is both startling and completely intoxicating, and I can't hold back the small gasp that slips past my lips.

He chuckles low, turning to place his face at my neck while his other hand passes over and unbuckles my shorts with a quick twist of his fingers.

His thumb burns a path along the waistband, causing me to

Chapter 8

shudder against him. "Tell me. Have you slipped your hand down here and imagined it was me?"

Yes. God, yes.

My chest heaves up and down as my eyes do a quick glance at our surroundings. The high plastic sides make it impossible to see in while the umbrella-like top shields us from those above.

"Words, Aria." His stern voice vibrates along my collarbone, and I nearly moan at the deep sound. "Would you like me to show you how nothing you've pictured amounts to the real thing?"

Somehow, I focus through the building haze. "Yes. If you think you can manage the challenge."

"*Hmph.* Let's see if you can keep that same fire with my fingers buried inside you."

My pussy clenches. His words, his demeanor, the sudden shift, all of it is doing things to my body faster than I can keep up with. Talking shit for years, having obvious sexual tension, and even throwing out not-so-subtle hints doesn't amount to the real thing. It's not the same when the annoying guy I've known my entire life isn't here. And in his place is a man with nothing but hunger and need staining his words while his hands are wrapped almost possessively around my body.

Kam moves as the third cabin empties, his finger sliding past the hem of my panties. "You say you can't stand me. That all I do is annoy the hell out of you. But I wonder if this cunt of yours will say the same thing? Or will I find her dripping with the truth?"

Rather than wait for a response, he nips at my neck while shoving two thick fingers inside of me. I can't stifle the gasp in time, which makes him smile against my throat.

Or maybe he smiles because I am, in fact, completely drenched.

Either way, it doesn't matter, because in the next second, Kam's lips are at my ear. "I knew it. You're such a little liar, Aria." He flicks his fingers once, causing me to jolt, and hooks his foot around my ankle. "Now, open up for me."

The stubbornness in me keeps my thighs closed around his hand, but then he curls his fingers and I relent, opening just enough for him to slide out comfortably.

"Attagirl." His voice is huskier than it was before, but I can't focus on that. I can't focus on anything because he spreads me farther, hoisting one of my legs over his thigh. "Let me take care of you."

My mind is going haywire, taken over by my libido and going into overdrive. Perhaps it's because I've tried to downplay what a sexual experience with him might be, but right now, I've never felt so damn good.

With every shift and pump of his fingers, my body melts into his. Meanwhile, the ride ascends and my heart beats harder. Every sense I have is heightened, tingling, yearning, and desperate for more.

I want to run my hands up his arms and feel the dip and ripple of his muscles. I want him to move his mouth back to my ear so I can hear his heavy breathing and see if it matches the pace of mine. I want to turn my head and see his face, decipher the look in his eyes, so I know if this is just him fulfilling a lost bet, or if he wants this just as badly as I do.

This time when my eyes squeeze shut, it's impossible to peel them back open. Kam's fingers are working me into delirium, hitting all the right spots—some of which I didn't know existed—while he casually talks shit.

"Tell me, Aria. What would everyone say about their chief of police if they saw how easily she came apart for me?"

"Fuck you," I manage to spit through clenched teeth, though my words still have less of a bite than I'd like.

Chapter 8

"All you have to do is say the word, sweetheart."

He drives his fingers deeper with the promise, forcing my back to arch off the seat, a moan slipping free. He slides his free hand up to my chest and presses me back down. "If I would have known you sound so sweet with my fingers in your cunt, I would have done this a long time ago."

I ignore his words, though it doesn't take much effort because his thumb finally finds my throbbing clit and begins doing lazy circles.

This time I'm able to swallow the needy whimper, but only just barely. "Ah, a man who knows where to find it."

Kam chuckles, his warm breath sprouting goose bumps as it coasts along my chest. The ride reaches the peak and Kam moves the hand on my chest up, wrapping it around the base of my neck. His fingers flex, squeezing the sides of my throat as his thumb starts moving faster. "After this, I'll be the last man who needs to find it."

I know his words are just meant to turn me on, but I can't deny the switch it flips inside of me. The notion of how much I *like* the thought. How much I *like* the command he has over me. Heat curls low in my stomach, tingles radiating up my limbs as the pressure starts to build. I lift one hand to grasp the one he has around my throat and grip his finger tighter. The air becomes harder to suck in, and soon my head starts to swim, adding to the mounting sensation between my thighs.

He hums, the sound of satisfaction driving me somehow higher than I already am. "I feel it. Go ahead and give it to me."

I bite into my lip so hard that the distinct taste of copper that follows doesn't surprise me. I'm not sure why I'm trying to keep from coming, maybe to prove a point or to be an asshole, but a few more passes and I won't have a say.

"I said, give it to me, Aria." He flicks his thumb faster while curling his fingers in a deadly KO. "*Now.*"

And just like that, the command paired with the twist of his digits is my undoing. I completely unravel. Wave after wave of my orgasm crashes over me, and I shamelessly hold on to Kam to keep me afloat. I must make a noise, but I'm too lost in euphoria to realize it until his hand shifts from my throat to cover my mouth.

It feels like an eternity before he slows his pace and takes his fingers away, leaving me empty and rebuttoning my shorts. My body mourns the loss of both him and his heat as I peel my eyes open and attempt to steady my breath.

"I was wrong about you, Firefly." Kameron's eyes are a blue blaze of fire washing away whatever doubt I had about how much he wanted me.

Still in an orgasmic haze, I can't form words in response, part of me still too stunned at what just happened to articulate my question. But when my lips finally part to ask him what he means, the door opens, and he exits without another word said.

Kameron
CHAPTER NINE

I take back what I said. I am an asshole. A stupid one at that.

Somewhere in my cerebellum, I thought that getting a taste of Aria would put my mind at ease. Show me there is no way the two of us were sexually compatible, and the tension between us was just that; regular, competitive tension.

I never thought I'd be *so* fucking wrong.

Sure, I had an idea that taking her on the Ferris wheel and confining us to the small space would turn into something—hopefully something that would ebb my curiosity for her—but I had no idea it would make me so much hungrier.

Not once did I consider that I would involve elements of my sexual nature. I didn't intend to play with her senses, and the reasoning behind it was simple; if she liked it, my goal of ridding me of the ivy on my wall would turn into allowing it to completely devour me. And I'd happily let it.

So for my sake and my sanity, it was going to be a straightforward one-night stand.

But then she went and licked the hot fudge.

It ignited a curiosity in me I couldn't shake, and my dumb ass just had to explore it further.

Kameron

When we were young, probably around eight or nine, our parents took us to a monster truck rally. Our tickets were kind of high up, but we had the best view of the whole arena. Aria and I stared in awe at all the trucks and it didn't take long before we were arguing about which one was best. Naturally, we had to make a bet on which of our trucks would win. I knew it would be the one that looked like a shark, but Aria was adamant it was going to be the one that resembled Frankenstein.

Everything was fine until the event started. Aria probably didn't even realize it, but before five minutes had even passed, the entire right side of her body was smooshed against mine, and her knuckles were white from gripping the edge of the bleacher. The loud sounds, the vibrating metal seats, the humid air, all of it was part of the experience that comes with a monster truck rally, but for her, she was overstimulated and it exacerbated a fear I wasn't aware she had until that day. Though at that age, all I was able to pick up on was the obvious —Aria was scared of heights.

Slowly, without calling attention to it, I slipped my hand between the very narrow space between our thighs and threaded my fingers on top of hers.

I remember the way she stiffened at my touch and the way I'm pretty sure my heart was going to fall out of my butt, but a minute passed and she relaxed. There were a few times she shifted at an extra loud part of the show or a big destruction display, but with my hand on hers, she was able to enjoy it.

Later that night, she came to collect my new bottle rocket.

"Too bad your truck lost," she'd said, her big brown eyes scanning the floor, watching as she dug the toe of her Vans into the sidewalk.

But for once, I didn't care that I'd lost. I was too busy staring at her right hand, the one clutched around the rocket.

Chapter 9

The one mine had held for two hours and still prickled with the memory.

When she noticed where I was looking, her cheeks bloomed a pretty pink and she hurried back home, a whispered thanks floating behind her.

There are two very distinct reasons I'm recalling the events of that night as I walk the carnival grounds toward the bonfire.

One being that same hand I held hers with, is the one I used to bring her to shambles, making it feel poetic in a way. And two, I used her fear of heights to do what I promised I would never do and played with her senses.

I didn't get on the ride expecting that to happen—teasing her while she was nervous, sure—but finger fucking her a hundred feet in the air was definitely not on my agenda.

What we did is completely out of my normal realm of what I'd consider sensory play, but toying with one's adrenaline—especially of the fear variety—makes for a much more intense sexual experience. Which, technically, *is* what this type of play is used for.

And not to toot anyone's horn, but I'm fairly certain Aria's experience was unlike anything she's ever had. Hell, even that small snippet was some of the most intense moments *I've* ever had.

The higher the Ferris wheel climbed, the tighter her grip was, and the harder she breathed. When my hand wrapped around her delicate throat, and she shivered beneath my touch, I almost lost it. But her reliance on me as her body ascended into her orgasm kept me grounded. All these things are par for the course, but because it was her—Aria Castillo—it felt different. It felt like *more*.

It was one time. It's over now.

The intrusive thought digs into my side, injecting me with a heavy dose of disappointment. My arms go slack at my sides, and my throat swells with what feels like dismay.

Why did I think that would be enough? Considering I've wanted that woman under me for the better part of a decade, I should have known better.

"Captain Ford. Are you ready?" One of my volunteer firefighters beams at me from across a stack of strategically placed wood.

I nod, stepping forward to ensure everything has been set up properly.

The large plot of land where we hold the carnival is near the outskirts of town, right next to a lake that stretches about half a mile wide. It isn't anything too extravagant, but the view is still stunning. Tall trees and patches of forest surround the east and west sides but are all far enough that any wayward embers would long die before reaching them. On the other side of the lake are houses, one of which belongs to Aria.

My heart squeezes. She's probably there now, complacent and satisfied, glad to finally get me out of her system.

I suck in a deep breath and crouch down. The dirt beneath is perfect, free of dry, dead leaves and instead leveled with moist dirt. Large stones around the stack act as a border, keeping people far enough away that they can't burn themselves but close enough that a long stick will be able to melt the perfect marshmallow for a s'more.

It only takes us a few minutes to get the fire going while everyone pulls out large blankets and sets up a little area with their families for the fireworks.

"Hey, I'm back. You can go." James's voice pulls me from a daze I didn't even know I was in.

Though we've never had an incident, every year, one of us sticks around during the bonfire and firework show to make

Chapter 9

sure nothing goes awry. The other one stays at the station in case there are any calls. While the last one enjoys the night off.

It just so happens that this year, it's my night off.

With how I'm currently feeling, though, I don't really think sitting on the couch and watching a rerun of *The Office* is going to hit the same funny bones tonight.

"I think I'll stay tonight. How about you enjoy the night?"

James lifts a brow. "What happened?"

I shake my head. "Nothing. I just don't really have anything to do tonight."

"I mean, you could go entertain the chief over there. I'm pretty sure with how she's looking into the fire, she's either going to hug it or fuck it, and I don't think either of those will end well."

My head snaps in the direction he points his chin and sure enough, Aria is on the side of the bonfire, a transfixed stare on her face.

As if on cue, my heart starts to hammer in my chest as I watch her. Her hands are tucked into her back pockets, while her pose of having one foot out to the side is meant to be casual. But I can see the undertones of tension in her shoulders. The slight sway in her body as she follows the dance of the flames. The hard swallow she takes when the wood crackles.

It's the wildness of the fire that draws her attention. The snap and flick of the flame. The pull of the warmth but fear of its magnitude. Of its power. I know because it's what draws me.

Nothing lures me like the blaze or makes me feel so alive.

At least... nothing used to.

My feet carry me as if they have a mind of their own, and soon I'm next to her. We stand in silence for a moment, both of us gazing into the fire while listening to the excitement buzzing in the air around us.

I'm not positive how much time passes, but by the time Lauren makes her third s'more for James, I decide it's probably best I leave Aria to herself.

"Good nig—"

"How about a wager?" Her voice cements my feet into the dirt.

"A wager?"

She keeps her gaze in front of her and nods slowly. The glow of the flames illuminates her face, highlighting a chickenpox scar she has just beneath her plush lips and a freckle on the bridge of her nose. It emphasizes the soft point of her ears and the slender curve of her neck.

All of these things I've noticed before, committed to memory even, just like everything else about her, but the way the fire paints her skin in an orange hue makes her look almost unreal.

It isn't until her brown eyes flash to mine that I realize the tightness in my chest is from me holding my breath.

This woman. This ivy. She will end me if I let her.

I pull my bottom lip between my teeth and attempt to focus on what she's just asked. "I'll never turn down a challenge from you. Can I ask why, though?"

Aria's gaze drops momentarily before a smirk curves one side of her lips. "On second thought, I'll propose the bet after."

My eyebrows draw together. "After what?"

"We finish what you started."

My breath catches in my throat, and not even the fake cough I produce can cover up my shock. "Did I not already do that?"

"That was what ten years of built-up tension leads to? Can't say I'm disappointed, per se, but I do feel a little led on."

I scoff and turn my body toward her. "Led on?"

"Should I grab you an ear wax extractor, Ford?"

Chapter 9

This coaxes a chuckle from my chest. "Oh, I can hear you just fine, Firefly. I'm just a little taken aback."

I take a step forward and watch as her mask of composure slips. She swallows hard and her nostrils flare, but it disappears in the next blink. "Well, if I'm being honest, I told Elise I'd at least get to sit on your face. So right now, this kind of feels—" She waves a hand in the small space between us. "Unfinished."

Now it's my turn to let the mask drop. Surprise and desire swirl in my chest, perhaps even a bit of an ego boost knowing she wants what I've thought of too many times to count.

I take the hand I've yet to use since the Ferris wheel and bring it to my mouth. Her heady scent is still on my fingers and I have to bite back a groan as I take my index finger and glide it along my bottom lip.

I try to resist but end up giving in, allowing my tongue to peek out and follow the same path.

The taste ignites my blood in a frenzy, and even though my mind—albeit somewhere far away and almost inaudible—is telling me to think twice, I nod.

"Let's rectify that then, shall we?"

Aria
CHAPTER TEN

I am a sex goddess.

A woman who is confident in her sexual capabilities and knows how to make a man crumble in less than five minutes.

I am Aria motherfucking Castillo, and I will not be nervous to sleep with a man that I've wanted to fuck for half my life.

"You okay over there? You kind of got quiet on me during your little confident booster mantra." Elise's voice streaming from my car's speakers brings me back to the conversation.

Had I said that last bit in my head?

After I called the station to make sure everything was quiet and let her know I probably wasn't coming by tonight, I dialed Elise. I tried to do a brief overview of what had happened, but she wanted every detail possible. She claimed it wasn't because she was a perv, but that she was trying to get a sense of the whole picture. Then she told me she should give me a ticket for public lewdness.

"Okay, so tell me what has you so bent out of shape. Clearly, the man knows what he's doing with his hands, so I'm pretty sure his mouth will be even better."

I scoff, running a hand through my hair, but it only makes it

Chapter 10

halfway because, between the sweat of working over a fryer and the *other* events, it's now a rat's nest. "This was about getting ammo to use against him for the rest of the year while also proving to myself that he didn't want me all those years ago because he sucked at it."

Elise's laugh echoes off her bathroom walls. She's got me on speaker as she gets ready to go out to the Red Velvet. "Okay, a couple of things. One, maybe he did suck at it back then. But more importantly, have you ever thought that maybe you guys have been nervous about taking things there because both of you got some feelings tucked up in that rivalry of yours?"

I nearly scream my sarcastic laughter in response. "Kam is one big asshole."

"Is he? Besides the occasional cheating he does to win one of your bets, he's a pretty stand-up guy. He's kind, and respectful, he has you on your ass laughing every time we go out and stares at you like he would give you the damn moon on a skewer if you asked. Not to mention when we were kids, he always had your back. Whether it was holding your book bag when you complained it was too heavy, or letting himself get soaked so you could use his umbrella. You both just like to go toe to toe and enjoy challenging each other. There's nothing wrong with that. It's your personality. And it damn sure doesn't mean there can't be something more than sex, Aria."

My fingers tighten on the wheel as I turn into my driveway. More than just sex. Is that why I'm nervous? I mean, it damn sure would explain the constant flight of butterflies in my stomach and the way my heart pounds just from thinking of him.

What if it isn't about the sex and more about opening a door I've been too stubborn to acknowledge until now?

"How about we see how the head goes and we talk about the possibility of feelings later?"

Aria

Elise hums her approval. "Oh, for sure. I know you can teach an old dog new tricks, but it'd be nice if it already came knowing. From the sounds of it, though, I'd say you're in good hands."

I try but fail to ignore the flare of arousal when she mentions his hands. Between the way his fingers were gripped around my body, working my pussy like it was a full-time job, and then later stealing my breath, his hands are now a sexual trigger.

"Alright, I'm about to go in and take a shower because I feel gross and fairly certain I'll need two showers to wipe off the film of powdered sugar left behind."

Elise giggles. "Is it gross if I say leave a little of that film around your lips? It'll be like seasoning."

"Yes. You are disgusting. Good night. And don't forget to text me when you make it home safe or I'm showing up in the squad car."

"Yes, Mom."

I huff and use my most motherly tone. "Good girl."

"Hey, hey now, save the words of affirmation for Kameron. Something tells me that's his love language. Just make sure your voice is a little huskier."

We both break out in a fit of laughter, and just like that, the trepidation melts off my shoulders. After a quick goodbye, I pull into my garage and dart to my shower.

Kam and I agreed to meet at my place in half an hour, which is just enough time for a good shower, including a thorough shampooing. But also, he does have a spare key (because of being a lifelong friend and my parents approved designated person after Elise lost her spare in the lake), so I don't necessarily have to rush either.

When I peel out of my clothes and climb into the shower, it feels like walking under a waterfall. The hot water beats into

Chapter 10

my back, massaging my muscles with enough intensity that I can't even get lost in thought or stress myself out with wired nerves.

It's not until I hear Kam's voice right outside the bathroom that I realize I've been in the shower far past pruney.

"Hey, it's me. Do you mind if I borrow one of your plant hooks?"

"Not at all but be careful where you put my baby."

He chuckles. The sound is deep and moves low into my stomach. "I promise to be careful."

I hurry and do a final rinse, making sure all the conditioner is out of my hair before I get out and wrap a towel under my arms. It's when I'm squeezing the excess water from my hair that I hear the whirling sound of a drill. It's quick and only lasts about three seconds, but curiosity gets the best of me, and I'm out of the bathroom and into my room before he drops the tool.

Kam's blue eyes connect with mine, and a mischievous shimmer I've never seen before passes through them.

He also went home and showered, his blond strands still wet with the evidence. He's traded his tactical pants for gray sweatpants (of course) and a plain white *V*-neck that also must be made of that same magical non-ripping thread because it's holding the fabric steady over his broad chest.

His appearance is casual, one I've seen a bajillion times, but now, knowing what's about to happen, it makes all the blood in my body drive straight to my clit.

It's as though he's able to read my mind because he lays on his signature smirk.

My stomach flips and I have to force my face away to keep from blushing.

Why the hell am I blushing? I'm the sex goddess here who is about to fulfill a lifelong fantasy of suffocating a man with my glorious pussy. He should be the one with his nerves all jumbled.

I glance over my now disheveled sheets and see what he was doing. A thick black hook that I use to hold up one of my heavier pathos plants is now horizontally screwed into my wall about one foot above my headboard.

I open and close my mouth twice before I can form the question I'm searching for. "Are you a sadist?"

Kam laughs a full belly kind of laugh before realizing my brows are raised in waiting. He clamps his mouth closed, though his smile is still evident, and shakes his head. "No."

"Masochist?"

"Not at all."

"Deep into BDSM?"

His lip quirks, but he shakes his head again. "I wouldn't say deep, though what I'm into definitely falls into that category."

This makes me pause, and a quiver racks down my spine. Knowing he's *into* something makes this all the more exciting, and I can't even be bothered to shield my interest. I chew on my lip as I consider the different possibilities.

"Bondage?"

"Yes."

"Spanking?"

"Absolutely."

My cunt clenches around nothing. Then something a little far fetched comes to mind, something I saw a long time ago when exploring the deep web of porn. I shift on my feet and look down, which prompts Kameron to take a step toward me. He stops when I lift my head, leaving plenty of space between us. "Fire play?"

His eyes widen before they darken and it's then I realize whatever Kam is into, I'm going to like it very much.

"Where are your cuffs?"

Chapter 10

I motion with my chin behind him to the tall walnut dresser. "Top drawer."

He moves quickly, grabbing the requested pair and turning back to face me. When he does, there's a new fire in his eyes, the blue almost invisible from his dilated pupils. There's nothing left of the playful Kam who gambles in car rides and fresh-baked cookies.

No, the man in front of me is starved, and I'm the meal he's about to devour.

He takes one step forward. It's slow, calculated, and paired with the fact I'm in nothing but a towel while he's fully clothed, makes it all the sexier. "I am into something known as sensation play. I want to heighten your pleasure by stimulating and engaging your senses."

Another step and my heart leaps into my throat.

"There are many different ways to experience it, but some of my favorites include taking away or muting some senses to heighten others."

I lick my suddenly dry lips as he takes another step.

"Before I have my mouth on that sweet little cunt of yours, I need to know you're okay with it."

I hold my wrists out and nod a little too eagerly. "Yes. Absolutely."

He smirks and takes the final step to close the remaining distance between us. "If you're ever uncomfortable or want me to stop, just tell me."

I jerk when the cold metal connects with my hands, and it's then I realize how hot I am. My chest heaves up and down as he closes my wrists inside the cuffs, his warm amber scent both calming my nerves while driving my libido wild. I want to bury my face in his chest and surround myself with his smell.

He double-checks twice, making sure they're secure but not tight, and then deftly lifts them above my head and pins me to the wall. I let out a gasp at the sudden movement, which makes the corner of Kam's lip curl.

"Would you like me to tell you how this is going to go, or would you like it to be a surprise?" His voice is so deep and heady my clit throbs with his words. With his unspoken promise.

He keeps my hands above my head while his free hand plays with the edge of my towel. His touch is so featherlight, I can barely feel it, but the tingles that radiate from where his fingers brush against my flesh are addicting. I want more.

So much more.

My eyes close as he leans in, gliding his nose across my collarbone. Again, he applies light pressure, and when I arch into him, he huffs out a small laugh.

"You haven't answered my question, Aria." He moves along my neck and my arms break out in a gaggle of goose bumps.

"Tell me," I finally breathe.

My words are so faint I'm not even sure he hears me, but then I feel him smile against my throat.

"I'm going to finish my perusal of your neck, see if anything is particularly sensitive. Then I'm going to strip you of this towel and walk you to the bed. I'll have you face the wall and hoist your hands over the hook to keep you from touching me. With your permission, I'm going to place a satin blindfold over your eyes. And then, Firefly, I'm going to fuck you with my tongue until I risk drowning in your cum."

Aria
CHAPTER ELEVEN

By the time Kam's done talking, I can barely breathe. My entire body is throbbing, and there's an ache so deep in my core I could almost cry.

As promised, he continues to explore my neck and chest with the tip of his nose, the touch still so light it's borderline torturous. But during his thorough search, he finds two different spots I wasn't aware would make my knees buckle.

The first one is right below my ear, just before my jaw. A moan slips out when he passes over it, which prompts him to go back and kiss the spot.

His lips are so damn soft, and now all I can think of is how they'll feel between my thighs.

"Kameron." It's meant to be a command but comes out as a breathy request.

He continues exploring as he murmurs a quiet *hmm* in return.

I open my mouth to tell him just what I need when he finds the second spot. This one is at the curve where my neck meets my shoulder and my knees wobble so hard he has to use the hand not holding mine to steady me. With just the soft touch of his nose, he's somehow turned me on more than I've ever been in my life.

"Kam."

"Yes, sweetheart. Talk to me."

"I'm going crazy here."

He backs away and smiles softly, the dimple appearing near his laugh lines. "I can see that."

The teaspoon of annoyance that flutters through me with his cocky tone is all I need to regain some of my composure. "Kameron, if I'm not sitting on your face in the next thirty seconds—"

"Careful, Aria. You know I love a good challenge."

Irritation flares in my gut, but also, so does intrigue. He wants to take his time, explore my body and drive me mad in the process. While I appreciate the tact, I'm three seconds away from prematurely combusting, and I'm pretty sure my heart can't handle pounding away at this rate for much longer.

Instead of the biting remark I want to say, I tell him the unfiltered truth. "I need you."

His expression shifts from arrogant to surprise to desire all in a matter of seconds. He pulls his bottom lip through his teeth before his fingers flick open my towel and it drops to the floor.

I watch as Kam drags his gaze agonizingly slow up my body, burning a path the entire way. It's like I can physically feel exactly where his eyes are as they move, and I squirm in response. My breasts grow heavy, my nipples tighten so much it hurts, and by the time his eyes are back at my face, I'm barely able to stand.

He takes mercy on me at last, pulling me from the wall and guiding me to the bed. He releases my hands and sits first, moving directly in the middle, right under the hook, before motioning for me to join him.

With his guiding hand, I straddle either side of him, my

Chapter 11

hands the only thing in the way of our chests connecting. But having my bare pussy on top of his sweatpants is enough to steal the last bit of sanity I'm holding on to.

Kam is hard, like really fucking hard, and the massive bulge I feel pressing against my entrance makes my mouth water.

My hips move on their own, grinding down into his pelvis while my head falls back with a moan.

Why does dry humping this man feel so good? I could come like this. Holy shit... I *am* going to come like this.

Kam must know, too, because he spurs me on. "That's it, Aria. Just like that. Keep going."

He spent too long building my arousal, and now the heat is already budding and there's no way in hell I'm going to stop it.

He hisses through his teeth as I pass over his erection again and again. "You want to come? Come. Show me how bad you want to."

I press into him harder, rocking my hips faster so my throbbing clit gets just enough friction.

Something about the calm look on his face and the way his hands are fisting the sheets at his sides like he's one move away from snapping pushes me over the edge. My orgasm shoots through me unexpectedly, washing over me so powerfully I can't even find my voice. I try to continue to rock, to ride the wave, but whatever was holding Kam steady comes loose and his strong hands grip either side of my hips.

Without warning, he lifts me, ignoring the squeal of mixed shock and delight as he slides lower beneath me.

"Hook," he barks, and I follow his command immediately, tossing the cuffs around the metal hook, effectively securing my hands to the wall.

He must realize he's forgotten something because he grunts in frustration before digging his hand into his pocket. He yanks out a small black cloth, and it isn't until he unfolds it that I see it's the blindfold.

Pulling himself from under me, he quickly ties it around my eyes. The fabric is soft and blocks out everything completely. I can't even see the little light that was streaming from my bathroom door.

And just like Kam said, not being able to see or touch him has left me feeling incredibly vulnerable and, in turn, sensitive. My ears perk up, listening to the sheets ruffle as he positions himself back under me, while every small hair on my body is raised in awareness, waiting for him to brush against me.

When he finally does, my entire body jerks and a gasp slips out.

"I've got you." His voice is low and calm, but I can hear the visceral need lining every syllable, and somehow, my pussy throbs all over again. His fingers dig into my thighs as he puts them on either side of his face.

And when his warm breath coasts along the seam of my pussy, I can't stop the whimpers that flow freely from my lips. "Kam."

"Now," he groans, his voice so deep it vibrates up to my clit. "Fucking sit."

Heaven help me, I don't need to be told twice.

Since I can't see him, I lower slowly, dropping down until his nose skims along the side of my slit, sending jolts of unbridled pleasure through my limbs. I wait, thinking he'll adjust, but when he doesn't, I fight the waves of shivers and shift until I'm lined up perfectly with his mouth.

He rewards me with a long, languid lick through my seam and releases a guttural moan so deep I nearly buckle.

"*Kam.*" The desperate whimper in my voice would normally bother me, but right now, with *him*, I don't give a fuck.

Chapter 11

The moment he slid his fingers inside of me on the Ferris wheel, a part of me knew I was a goner. Seems as if my body had already known this fact and was just waiting for my head to catch up.

He hums against my clit and the sudden vibration makes me quiver, causing him to chuckle. At this point, it feels like a vibrator is a centimeter away from my clit and it's becoming worse than torture.

I lower myself more, pressing my pussy closer to his mouth. "Don't stop, Kameron."

He responds immediately, hooking both his arms under my thighs and gripping me right above the knee. He yanks me down harder, and with my hands secured above my head, I have no way to balance or fight against the sudden onslaught he unleashes on my cunt.

Holy shit.

Kam works me in three different ways at once, and with the inability to see him or touch him, I'm even more attuned to what he's doing. The curl of his tongue, the suction of his lips on my clit, the nibbles and soft bites. All of it is so intense, and I can do nothing but feel.

Feel him attack not only my body but my preconceived notions of what this was going to be like. What *he* was going to be like.

Kameron's fingers dig into my flesh as his tongue threatens to perform an exorcism on my soul. He interchanges between sucking and licking so smoothly, and it's only because of my heightened awareness that I'm able to pinpoint every minute change.

Moans fall freely now as I shamelessly ride his face, my orgasm somehow already building all over again. "Yes, right *there.*"

I want to touch him. To thread my fingers through his hair

and grip him closer to me. I want to run my hands all over him and absorb every ounce of pleasure he has to offer.

I yank against the cuffs, the same bites of pain from the metal burrowing into my wrists melt into pleasure with every pass of Kam's tongue.

The cold droplets that fall from my wet hair down my spine do nothing but accentuate the heat taking over everything. My body is too hot. My skin is too tight. Even without the ability to see, I feel the room starting to spin.

A tremor starts low, building into something so much more intense than before, and just as I start to climb to oblivion, Kam's hands disappear from my legs. In one swift motion, they are on my hips and lifting, snatching me from the hook and tossing me flat on my back. I start to open my mouth and call him an asshole, but the pure hunger in his voice stops me.

"I'm addicted already, Aria. Your taste..."

His heavy hands glide up the curves of my waist. "This body..."

One hand grips my chin between his thumb and forefinger. "*You.*"

My stomach flips at his words. I shouldn't like what he's saying or the way it turns my insides to complete mush, but fuck if it doesn't make my heart race and my pussy throb.

My feet hit the headboard as Kam comes down, sliding back in place between my thighs. He kisses my throbbing clit, chuckling when I yelp at his unexpected move. "I want all your little whimpers."

Another kiss, this one right at my entrance, making me tense. "I want all your shivers and cries of pleasure."

His tongue slides through my slit, and I nearly convulse. "I want it all. Every last drop. And you're going to give it to me."

Without waiting another second, he picks up right where

Chapter 11

he left off. Only this time, his fingers curl inside my entrance, finding my G-spot as if he's memorized exactly where it's at.

My fingers dive for his hair, threading through the damp strands and yanking him forward. I'm not sure what I want more at this moment—to let him finish his feast or urge him to push inside of me.

And then there's the tingle at my lips that wants to finally kiss him. See if it's as explosive as everything else.

His fingers work in tandem with his wicked tongue, causing heat to coil in my core. It only takes a minute before the build overwhelms me. I try to move, to shift away from the intense feeling, but Kam grips me tighter, holding me in place.

"Don't you fucking run from me, Aria." His words are barely audible over the blood racing through my ears.

Then, he sucks my clit into his mouth, effectively shoving me into the abyss and leaving me shaking from the intense fall. Though I'm sure it's only seconds, it feels like an eternity before my core stops pulsing and the haze finally settles. My breathing takes even longer to return to normal after making sounds resembling a dying animal. Sounds nobody has ever drawn from me before.

But when it finally does, I feel a bit of irritation sneak in. "All this time wasted betting on sports or how many shots James can take before he hits on a lamppost."

My voice is low and still breathy, but the statement makes Kam chuckle. He presses a soft, lingering kiss to my thigh, making me jolt slightly before he moves from between my legs. "What do you mean?"

Though I want to ask him where in the world he's going, I focus on what I'm more upset about. "We could have been betting to see who could make who come first. Or how hard. Or hell, I don't know... how many rounds you could go before you couldn't get it up anymore."

Now Kam breaks into a full-blown belly laugh and I twist, suddenly needing to see his face. He gets to the blindfold before I do and slips it off slowly. "I can find a few things wrong with that."

He pauses, almost as if he knows my eyes are readjusting before continuing. When his gorgeous blue irises come into view, I can't help the way my lips curve up at the edges. I lift my bound wrists, dropping them around his neck. "Hey."

Kam smirks, his gaze dropping briefly to my lips before meeting my eyes again. "Hey, Firefly."

I'm fairly certain my heart skips a few beats, but I don't let it show as I start to sit up. He helps me the rest of the way, unhooking my wrists from around his neck. It's hard to ignore the subtle drop of his shoulders now that we're no longer attached. "Tell me at least one thing?"

"Well for one," he starts, standing and returning to my dresser drawer. "I will *always* make you come harder. Every time."

I ignore his use of the word will and kick my feet over the side of the bed. "It's funny how you can make that assumption without having seen what I'm capable of."

Kam finds the little key to the cuffs and spins around. He falls to his knees in front of me, pushing my legs apart so he can position himself between them.

The sight of him like this—still fully clothed and sweat glistening at his temple while looking up at me with all the lust in his eyes—is so damn sexy my pussy clenches again. I blame it on the fact he hasn't filled her up yet and not that I'm already sex obsessed with this man.

He moves smoothly, unlocking the cuffs and rubbing my wrists as they drop free. The soft caress of his thumb against my tender skin is even sexy.

Chapter 11

"I'll admit you got me there. But still, I stand firmly with what I said. Too bad it doesn't matter, though."

My brows knit together as he reaches over and grabs my discarded towel. "What do you mean?"

Kam stands, that stupid, cocky, yet much too handsome grin on his face. "You wanted to sit on my face. You did. My job is done." He motions to my floor-to-ceiling windows. My house backs up to the lake, giving me the perfect view of the carnival on the other side. "Fireworks are going to start in about eight minutes. I'm sure you want to watch those, huh?"

Fucking men. I swear on everything, I'm about to throw a pillow at his face if he thinks he's leaving here without fucking me.

Sounds greedy, considering I've had three orgasms in the span of a couple of hours, but having felt what he's been hiding under that damn uniform, I refuse to not get the whole Kameron Ford experience. Especially if this is a one-time deal.

My heart squeezes at the thought. *Shit.*

Have you ever thought that maybe you guys have been nervous about taking things there because both of you got some feelings tucked up in that rivalry of yours?

Elise's words assault me as Kam leans down and presses his lips to my temple. It's a goodbye kiss. I don't want him to go.

Before I can give my internal ramblings much thought, I give in to the tight pinch in my chest. "Before you go... how about one last bet?"

Kameron

CHAPTER TWELVE

If I could jump for joy and not look like a complete idiot, I most certainly would. She wants me to stay. I mean... I think. Her exact words were, "If I can get you to come before the fireworks start, *you* have to make me come one more time."

Which is short for *she wants me to stay*. At least, that's my story, and I'm sticking to it because it's clear now; having reservations with her *was* time wasted.

All this time, I thought I couldn't keep the ivy attached to my walls because I would either have to change it or be overrun by it. And with how I feel—how I've always felt for her—I knew I would give up being in control just to be with her.

But now, there's nothing in the way of taking her. Not after I "cheated" and pretended I was about to leave.

I wanted to know if she felt the same. If the thought of not being with me made her a little desperate, like how she's made me feel. And it worked.

Her entire body tensed, she inadvertently put her hand out to stop me, and her pupils dilated as she searched for a way to get me to stay. That's all I needed to know that Chief Aria Castillo is *mine*.

Chapter 12

I readjust on the bed and lean my back against the headboard. She told me to give her a second before she ran out and disappeared into the kitchen. Watching her ass as she walks off has always been my favorite pastime, but seeing her do it naked? My second favorite thing in the world.

The first is watching her come undone for me.

Aria reappears in the doorway with a small white ceramic bowl in hand. She snatches the cuffs from the floor and tosses them at my chest. "On."

I lower my eyelids, gazing at her with a challenging smirk on my face. "Should I get the blindfold too?"

She beams, moving closer and setting the bowl on the nightstand. "Yes. But hurry it up. I only have about fifteen minutes."

"Fifteen?"

Aria's smile turns into a deviously sneaky little grin. "I may have sent a quick text to buy me a little more time."

I scoff. "And you say you don't cheat."

Her eyes narrow. "Put them on now."

"Yes, Chief Castillo," I relent, doing as told. It's not like I want her to lose this bet, so I'm damn sure not going to argue about it.

Within thirty seconds, I'm blindfolded with my wrists cuffed and secured around the same hook. It's extremely rare that *I'm* on the receiving end of having my senses played with, and to say my nerves feel like lightning would be an understatement. My heart hammers into my sternum as I feel the mattress dip down with her weight. She shuffles across the bed, and soon, she's straddled across my waist again.

Even through my sweatpants, I can feel the heat of her cunt. It sends my pulse into a race, whooshing through my ears so fast I barely hear her tell me to lift my hips.

She yanks my sweats down just enough to free my throbbing cock, and I can't lie, the soft gasp she lets out when she sees it is extremely satisfying.

"What's wrong, sweetheart?" My tone is a little cocky, but it wouldn't be me if it wasn't.

I can't see her, but I know she's giving me a death stare. "Not a problem at all. Just thought it would be a little bigger."

An unexpected chuckle escapes my chest. "Did you? Sorry to disappoint. But you know what they say? It's not the size that matters, but how they use it."

"So they say." Her voice is meant to be calm, sarcastic even, but I can hear the trepidation lining her words.

I bet she gets forty percent of it in her mouth before she gags.

After a few seconds of nothing, I tilt my head to the side. "You're running out of time, Aria. Everything okay?"

"Of course. I just don't think I'll need that long."

"Oh? And why is th—"

I suck in a harsh breath as her cold mouth covers the head of my cock. The sudden temperature shift after being warm for so long is jarring but feels so fucking good that my exhale is a groan.

I must have been too busy focused on what she was doing that I didn't hear her playing with ice in her mouth, but *oh my fuck*, do I feel it now.

Aria swirls her tongue around the top before sliding down, and already my blood is pumping too fast. Sucking on her way back up, she then flicks her way to the base, stopping halfway to breathe. She runs her cool tongue along my shaft, coaxing more guttural sounds from my chest. For the first time in my life, I'm glad I can't see her because I'm pretty certain I would have come already. She moans around me and my muscles tense. "God, you take me so well, Aria."

She tries to move down again, this time going farther, and

Chapter 12

when her throat muscles seize around my cock with her gag reflex, I nearly convulse. The sound is music to my ears, and I can't help but praise the effort. "That's it. Relax your throat for me, sweetheart."

One of her hands grips my upper thigh while the other finds the base of my dick. It's wet and cold, and I realize she must have had ice in the bowl as well. I twist my hands in my cuffs, inviting the slight pain as they dig into my wrists.

Her mouth has already begun to warm up, and as she works my cock up and down, the drastic change in temperature has me panting. She rotates her hand counterclockwise, squeezing as she sucks all the way to the tip.

"Fuck, Aria. *Yes.* God, your mouth feels so fucking good."

She hums her contentment around me and the sensation surges through my balls. She's right. Having already done so much and built up the anticipation, there's no way I'm going to last.

Again, she goes down, and this time, I hit the back of her throat. Lightning shoots up my spine and I decide I can't do this. I need to be buried inside her the first time I come with her.

I jerk my hands down hard. The hook pops from the wall, freeing me up to yank Aria up by her shoulders. She releases my cock with a wet pop, a surprised gasp escaping her.

"I need you on my cock, Firefly." I rush out the words as I manage to pull her back into a seated position over my hips. "I need *you.*"

I rip the blindfold from my eyes and grab either side of her face. The moment her eyes drop to my lips, I smash my mouth against hers.

No part of the kiss is tentative or sweet but hungry and full of pure need. It's years of snide comments, backhanded compliments, flirty passes, and missed chances. It's angry and passionate, and it isn't until we're both out of breath that we finally break away.

Our eyes meet for a brief second, and the intensity and fire blaring in her brown irises remind me of a blaze threatening to take me under. They promise danger and thrill. Euphoria and satisfaction.

Her hands glide up my chest, her touch leaving a searing path in its wake. "Tell me what else you need, Kam. I want to hear everything."

It's her this time that collides her lips with mine, and soon, her nails are raking over my shoulders in a needy attempt to pull at my shirt. Moving from her mouth, I leave a trail of kisses down her jaw to her neck. I nibble and lick my way to her ear before I tell her what I've wanted to say for way too damn long.

"I need to fill this tight little cunt until you're screaming." I bite her earlobe and revel in the shiver that racks down her body. "Until you're fucking weeping."

She whimpers against me, her fingers threading through my hair and scratching my scalp. "If I don't fucking cry from coming, I'm talking shit until Christmas."

I smirk, but the challenge sparks a new fire inside of me. "Get me out of these fucking cuffs, Aria."

Her eyes flare, the desire evident in the way she bites into her lip before scrambling off of the bed and grabbing the key from the dresser. We get the cuffs off in record time, along with my shirt and sweatpants. I grab a condom from my pocket before tossing them to the floor.

She giggles as I frantically pull her back on top of me while ripping open the small package.

"I'm going to fuck you twice, Aria." I fist myself as I roll the condom down and then grab either side of her hips. "The first time will be rough and fast because if I'm not filling this cunt

Chapter 12

up in the next four seconds, I'm going to fucking break something."

"*I* will break someth—*ahh*." I yank her down hard, impaling her with my cock and stealing the rest of her sentence with my mouth.

She bites down on my lip, a desperate whimper matching the low grumble of mine.

It takes a moment for us to adjust to the feeling of me inside her. She's wrapped around me like a custom-made glove while her arousal and heat are sending my mind into a daze.

It isn't until both our breaths have slowed just a fraction that I lift her hips, bringing her halfway up my shaft, and then slam her back down.

She screams out at the same moment the first firework explodes outside. Bright colors of reds, blues, and whites paint her frame the shining colors. I lift her again but pause to tell her what comes next. "Then I'm going to fuck you slow. Take my time and learn what senses you like played with the most."

She shivers around my words. Around my promise. And while every single cell inside my body is burning to hurry up and take her, there's one last thing I need from her before I can.

"One more thing."

Her gaze finds mine, and the sparkling colors of the fireworks reflecting in her eyes give me pause. It's in this moment, right here, that I know I never want to look at fireworks any other way.

Despite my nerves and a small part of my ego telling me I shouldn't put myself out on a limb for her to chop down, I say what I've longed to for over a decade.

"This is it for me, Aria. I need you to know that after this, you're mine. And I will take any challenge or bet to keep you."

It could very much be the flash of fireworks outside, but I

swear a sheen crosses over her eyes. "So you want to play for keeps?"

There's an undeniable hope in her words, and I have to stifle the smile itching to break free. "Yes."

She bites into the corner of her lip. "Then let's play."

It's hard to contain the smile begging to break free, but then she shifts and my cock demands attention.

My grip on her hips must be bruising, but the way we lose ourselves to each other, I doubt it matters. I begin to thrust my hips up while guiding her bounce, both of our hips meeting in aggressive slaps.

It doesn't take long before I can already feel her muscles tightening. "This pussy was made for me, Aria."

She moans her response, pausing her pace as she tries to slow her impending orgasm.

I shake my head, and in one fluid motion, I flip us, tossing her on her back and yanking her to the edge of the bed. I grab one of her pillows and shove it under her hips.

"So, about that bet. I'm cooking you dinner tomorrow night if you can hold your orgasm until I tell you. If you can't, I'll order in."

"I mean, it's a win-win either way, but I doubt it will be hard." She gives an overly ambitious smirk as I line myself back up.

"I beg to differ."

I slam inside of her hard, relishing the strangled gasp that leaves her mouth. I drive in and out of her, again and again, pulling all the way out before driving back inside. Her legs tighten around my waist while her hands grasp wildly at the sheet beside her. She's so close.

"That didn't take long." I lean forward, pinching one of her nipples before grabbing her low at her throat. "But I didn't say you could come. You really want to lose that quickly?"

Chapter 12

"I didn't expect you to feel so damn good, Kam."

I lift an amused brow. "Is that right?"

"Yes," she hisses.

"Oh, you're a pretty little liar, aren't you, Firefly?"

"Semantics, Kam. Just don't you dare fucking move."

I can't help the chuckle that rumbles across my chest. I squeeze her throat harder while moving my other hand to sit right above her pelvis.

"Do me a favor and come on my dick, sweetheart." I press down on her stomach and drop my thumb to rotate over her swollen clit.

"Holy fuck, Kameron." Her voice is garbled as she bucks against the intense sensation.

Almost as if on cue, the finale to the fireworks show starts, lighting the sky and her room in dozens of colors.

"Oh, my... fuck, *fuck*. Please, *please* don't sto—" She never gets to finish begging because she explodes.

Her pussy squeezes the life out of my cock as it convulses while her cries of ecstasy act as a catalyst that sets my entire body alight. I follow right behind her, coming harder than I ever have before, and continue driving into her until we're both spent.

I'm not sure how much time passes after I collapse on top of her to catch my breath. It could be a minute or even an hour before I notice the fireworks fade into nothing. Maybe because I'm lost in the sound of her racing heart, or content as she runs her hands up and down my spine. But either way, I could stay in this moment forever and wouldn't miss a thing.

"Technically, I won," she finally says.

Her voice is so sated, I would smile if I wasn't already laughing. I stand slowly, careful when I pull out of her.

She winces as she sits up, and when she notices my

triumphant smirk, she rolls her eyes. "I'll get you the recipe of what I want cooked and ready when I get off tomorrow."

"You didn't win."

"You said I could come. So I win. Don't be a sore loser."

"Fine. But I don't need your recipe." I cup one side of her face and rub my thumb along her jaw.

The light seeping from the bathroom illuminates her face in a soft glow, a hard contrast to the vibrant colors that have been playing over her skin. Her lips are swollen from our kiss, her tan skin is flush, and her damp hair is mussed, falling over her face in beautiful waves. "You're so goddamn stunning."

I don't mean to say it out loud; we both know she doesn't need the ammo, but fuck do I mean it. We both knew opening this door would be trouble. Knew that it would probably do more harm than good. But never did I expect her to be such a perfect match. Such a perfect fit.

So I tell her. Because why not? She's mine after this, and she needs to know how I feel without all the sarcastic bullshit filtering in between.

"Just perfect."

"Kam." She tries to turn her face so I can't see her smile, but it's too late, I've seen her.

Truly seen her. In all her ferocity, passion, and bliss.

And now, it's time she gets to see me. "Now, I need you to be a good girl and do exactly what I say. I'm not done exploring you yet."

Aria
CHAPTER THIRTEEN

Somehow, despite my legs feeling like Jell-O, I manage to walk to the bathroom and complete the task of taking a quick shower while Kam sets up the room. What all that entails, I have no idea, but it's left my nerves somewhere between excited and mystified.

Hell, *everything* this man is doing and saying has my body on edge in the best way. It's why I've braided my hair to the side—another request—and slipped on a matching black set of lace underwear. And because I want to feel like a present that he has to unwrap, I've also thrown on an oversized white shirt.

Glancing in the mirror one last time, I notice that besides my flushed cheeks, courtesy of the hot shower, I don't look half-bad. Especially for having just been railed within an inch of my life.

I chuckle to myself. Elise is going to have a field day with me.

See, there have been many occasions when she and I have considered what Kam would be like in bed. I figured a lot of fighting and switching, neither of us being able to agree on who should be in control. While she said he would completely dominate me.

I laughed her off every time, considering who I am and my need to constantly be in control. Funny, how in the end, she was right.

With *him*, I don't need to do that. I don't need to put in extra effort or dictate his every move in order to feel good. On the fucking contrary.

He's taking his time to learn my body, searching every inch with delicate touches and soft kisses. He wants to find out what makes my toes curl and my limbs shiver, relieving me of the need to teach him.

That alone makes me like him a whole lot more. I mean, I know at some point I'll probably have to sock him in the eye for him being an ass, but in the bed? He can command every last inch of me, and I won't say a word. If I'm being completely honest, should this man say he's serious about us being something, I will make him coffee every morning like it's my damn job after what he's doing to me.

"Ready when you are, Firefly." Kam's low voice seeps through the bathroom door and travels straight into my core.

I smile, rubbing my hands together like a greedy little orgasm gremlin before opening the door.

In the ten minutes I was gone, Kam transformed my room into a safety hazard. There are candles everywhere, on almost every flat surface, and the entire space is glowing like a séance is about to occur. My bed has been stripped, leaving only the fitted sheet and what appears to be fuzzy cuffs—for both my ankles and wrists—attached to long cords that run beneath my mattress. In the center is an oversized mint-colored satin blindfold.

The entire scene looks like something from that book with the gray tie, but I can't deny the very heavy feeling that moves low into my stomach. My eyes find Kam, who is leaning against

Chapter 13

my dresser, hands crossed over his still naked chest, (though he put back on the sweats), and next to him...

Unexpected laughter escapes me as I point down at his feet. "Kameron. A fire extinguisher? I'm not sure if I should be scared or more turned on."

He smirks—the cocky one I'm starting to appreciate—and drags his bottom lip through his teeth. "Well, for tonight, it's a precaution for the candles."

Kameron kicks off the dresser and takes a weighted step toward me. "But in the future, it's a precaution for me."

My stomach does that stupid flip thing while my clit gains a pulse from the sudden rush of blood. "For you?"

He nods, taking another step. "Yes. In the future, I plan to take your love, or perhaps infatuation with fire, and bring it here."

I gulp, and I'm fairly sure it's audible. "Here?"

"You sound like a parrot now. Yes, sweetheart, here. But for now, I just want to give you a massage."

"A massage with a happy ending, right?"

He closes the remaining distance and tips my chin up with his pointer finger. His amber scent invades my nose, and it takes far too much energy to focus on his words. "Of course. This shirt has no sentimental meaning to you, does it?"

I shake my head.

"Good."

Before I can utter a word, Kam does exactly what I intended, grabbing the fabric and ripping the shirt from my body with one easy pull.

And there she goes.

If it wasn't for the grand show of masculinity, it's the need in his hooded gaze as he takes in my underwear of choice. My skin tingles as he soaks in the little details, and when he reaches a hand out to trace the rim of my bra, my body breaks out in goose bumps.

"That light touch thing you do is going to be the death of me."

Kam's eyes flash to mine. "Death by orgasm. Sounds like a good way to go."

He grips me by my hips and literally tosses a giddy me on the bed, right next to the blindfold. It's a pretty mint green, but also the color of the envy swelling in my chest. I wonder how many women he's used these on before.

"Like it?" He asks, tucking his hands in his sweats.

I nod, too scared my voice will betray me. I mean, we literally just started a sexual exploration marathon a couple of hours ago, so it's definitely not my business nor my right to be jealous. Besides, it didn't bother me with the black one—

"I got it a while back. Saw they had them in your favorite color and had to get it."

My brows knit together. "You knew my favorite color?"

I shouldn't be surprised considering we've known each other our whole lives, but you'd be astonished at the things people don't pay attention to.

He rubs at the nape of his neck. "Yeah. I hoped maybe one day we'd get to use it."

I'm not sure how I'm supposed to feel knowing this man—the one I fight with on a weekly basis due to his inability to win a bet fair and square—purchased something for me in hopes of using it during sex, but I'm all the way turned on.

"Where do you want me?"

Kam smiles and juts his chin toward the center. "On your stomach. Legs and arms out."

I bite into my lip and do as told, pushing the blindfold to the side. When I position myself as he's instructed, I hear the

Chapter 13

moment he realizes my panties are made for moments like these.

The black lace has an extra row of fabric above the waistband, arching over my ass to accentuate my curves. While near my pussy, it's been made with a perfect-sized hole, allowing for penetration without needing to take them off.

He tsks, running his hands along the backs of my legs until he reaches under my butt. His fingers grip into the soft flesh as he pushes my legs apart. "Here I thought you were a sweetheart when really you'd rather be my slut."

Holy fuck, why does that sound so hot?

"And look at this." My body jerks as he swipes a finger through my seam. "You're already fucking soaked for me."

"*Kam.*" My voice is barely a whisper.

His large hands return to the back of my thighs and I shudder while he works his way down to my ankle. He takes his time attaching the restraints.

"None of tonight will cause you any pain, but if you are ever overwhelmed, or overstimulated, just tell me, and I'll stop. Do you understand?"

"*Yes,*" I breathe.

He pops me on the ass. It doesn't hurt, but the way the vibrations move down to my clit, I have to bite my tongue to keep from telling him to do it again, only harder.

"That's my girl." He works his way up, running his calloused palms up my back and over my arms.

When he gets to my wrists, he secures them and then tightens it, leaving me completely and utterly bared to him. My pulse thumbs under the heat of his gaze as he checks over the locks. I've never felt so sexy and aroused in my entire life, and honestly, I'm more nervous I won't be able to last before I become a puddle of cum.

He leans over the bed and grabs one of the candles. It's one of the few that aren't lit and in a container with an odd spout.

"This candle is actually a massage oil. It doesn't burn as hot and when I drip it on your skin, I'll use it to massage you." Kam moves on top of me, widening his legs so they rest on the outside of mine. He's overly gentle as he picks up my braid and puts it on one side of my shoulder. "I'm going to start here but then work my way down. When I get to your lower back, I'll be putting the blindfold on you."

"Okay." My voice is a little louder, and my heart has calmed a fraction now that I know what to expect.

I watch in my periphery as he tilts the container and the first bit of wax pours out. When it connects with my skin, I immediately arch my back—though not much due to the restraints—and moan at the incredible warmth of it.

The temperature is perfect, kind of like a Jacuzzi in the middle of February, and it makes the rest of my body shiver from being so cold in contrast.

Kam must sense it because he lowers himself, covering my bottom half with his sweats before he sets the candle down and starts massaging my shoulders.

God, I want to berate myself for not doing this sooner. His hands are like magic, kneading into every tight muscle, every nook and cranny. I melt under his touch, moans and whimpers falling freely as he works my entire back.

He does this again and again, pouring, then massaging while working down until he's at the top of my ass. As promised, he puts the blindfold over my eyes before starting down below.

Now the sensation feels different. I'm not sure if he's grabbed another candle, but the wax is hotter. Nowhere near uncomfortable, but when it drips right below the curve of my

Chapter 13

ass, my entire body shifts. I can no longer see him either, so when the wax falls, it's a more intense sensation.

"You're so incredibly soft, Aria." His hands glide under my panties with ease, and he rubs my ass for a while before his sneaky little hands slide over to my pussy. He stays on the outside of my slit, moving up and out, spreading my lips so he can hear my slickness.

And I am soaked. I'm pretty sure there's a spot surrounding me now with how badly I want him inside me. Hell, I'm damn near trembling. But what he's doing now, building me up with every touch and knead, is a paradise I need to prolong.

"Before I go down to your calves, I need a quick taste." He gives the warning, but it isn't enough for me to prepare for the flat of his tongue to slide through my seam.

I nearly jump out of my skin, screaming an obscenity into the mattress as he does it four more times. My pussy throbs and pulses as he moves his tongue and the torture of his slow pace is what I assume is one of the levels of the underworld.

What was I saying about paradise? Give me hell. "Fuck me, Kameron."

He pauses his tongue and the mattress dips as he sits back up. "What was that, sweetheart?"

"I don't want to be your sweetheart right now," I choke out, squirming impatiently under him. "I want you to fuck me."

I hear the candle thud against the wood nightstand as he drops it down. "But we haven't gotten to the other things I had planned."

"*Please*, Kam."

I hear the damn smirk in his voice. "Are you begging for my cock, Chief Castillo?"

Normally I would berate him for his arrogant-ass tone, but right now, all I can think about is feeling him again. "*Yes*. Please. I need you inside me."

At first, I think he's going to make me beg a little more, but the telling rip of a condom package is music to my aching core.

"Since you asked me so nicely." He tugs my braid free before moving between my knees. Then leaning back, he loosens the cuffs around my ankles.

"What about these?" I wiggle my wrist lightly to remind him I'll be stuck in this position if he leaves them. Not like I mind, though.

"Do you want me to fuck you like my slut?" He moves to put both hands on either side of my hips.

"Yes." It's a heady moan as I arch my back, lifting my ass as high as the restraints allow.

"Then they stay on."

One of his hands disappears, and at first, I think it's to help line himself up, but then the sharp pop of his dick slapping against my swollen clit makes me scream out in surprise.

"*Kam.*"

The low grumble of his chuckle makes me wish I could buck back harder than the feeble attempt I give, only making him laugh more. But when I start to squirm in impatience, he pushes inside of me.

My moan matches the loudness of his satisfied hiss as he pauses to let my pussy stretch to accommodate him.

In this position, with my legs on the outside of his, he's hitting spots that have never been touched—not even by ol' faithful in my top drawer.

I whimper as he goes deeper, and he rubs either side of my hips. "You can take it, sweetheart."

Tingles light up my body at his words, and I arch my back a little more while he buries himself to the hilt. "Fuck, Firefly. You feel so goddamn good."

Somehow, despite the slight ache in my cunt, my sex goddess makes an appearance. "Show me how good I feel."

Chapter 13

He huffs a small laugh as he slowly slides out of me. "That's my girl."

Then he slams into me, *hard*. I bury my face back into the mattress and Kameron fucks me senseless. He isn't moving fast, but the intensity in every thrust rattles me to my core each time his hips slap against my ass.

"God, you take me so well." Again and again, he barrels into me. One of his fists wraps around my hair to pull me back slightly. "I told you. Perfect fit."

The telling warmth and tingles build low in my belly as he continues driving into me over and over. But then, out of seemingly nowhere, I hear it. The soft buzz of my handy sidekick.

It's the only warning I have before the head of my vibrator meets my swollen clit. He taps it against me to match the rhythm of his thrusts and I swear the fireworks display has started all over again.

I scream out, the pressure building faster, and soon, I'm shaking with the impending explosion.

"There it is. Come on my cock, Aria," Kam coaxes, and my body responds immediately.

My pussy contracts with every mind-altering pulse while flashes of color appear behind the blindfold. I'm panting, barely able to keep my body arched, as Kam finds his own release with a guttural moan. We fly together, and by the time we've ridden every throbbing wave, we are nothing but a mess of tangled limbs and slick bodies.

We lie in blissful silence for a while, only our steadying breaths and racing hearts filling the quiet air. But after a few minutes, Kameron unlocks the soft cuffs and pulls me onto his chest, slipping off the blindfold.

His blue eyes bore into me with a soft intensity I've never seen before, and I'm almost certain my lungs are no longer working at full capacity.

He brushes a wayward strand of hair from my face. "I meant what I said about playing for keeps. I've wanted you for so damn long, and now, after this, it proves I haven't just been imagining how perfect we'd be."

I remain quiet as he strokes the side of my face and searches my eyes for something to give away just how big my heart is currently swelling. "You've embedded yourself in me. From your wit, smart-ass mouth, charismatic nature, and your absolute perfect ass. The prettiest firefly I've ever seen, and I'm yours if you'll have me."

If I'll have him? He has no idea.

I suppress the telling twitch in my lips and poke him in the chest lightly. "About that meal you have to make me. I think I'll take Hibachi."

Kam's hand drops from my face but he nods, a soft smile on his lips. It almost tortures me to see him so pouty. "Yes, ma'am. Anything else?"

"Yeah," I sigh, pressing a long, tender kiss to his lips. "I need to know how you take your coffee."

Aria

EPILOGUE
ONE YEAR LATER

"And remember not to pose a risk to others by overloading your sockets. You have to consider too many factors, most of which are unknown, that will affect the likelihood of an electrical fire."

"Like what?" a girl seated toward the front of the room asks. She'll be a freshman at Stanford University in California this fall.

Kam paces as he lists the various issues with dorms. "Well, the age of the building, for one. Capacity. Whether it's being maintained. There are also factors such as climate, geography, and surrounding buildings. So it's best to have a plan no matter where you are."

I smile as I watch Kam conduct his fire readiness speech with the girls. He did it last December when we got my classes up and running, and since, I've realized watching him talk about fire is one of my favorite things to do.

Probably because it reminds me of the speeches he gives while setting my back on fire in different shapes during our rare fire fleshing adventures.

I leave him to finish his class and join Elise in the back room. We've had the studio open for eight months now and

Epilogue

have learned a lot. Things we need that we didn't think we would, or stuff we never use. We make a list and price things out while delegating what's most important.

Later, when I hear Kam dismiss the girls, I hurry and file the papers away. We haven't told each other what we're raising money for this year—partially because we know the other will buy it.

I spin on my heels just as he reaches out for me, wrapping his arms around my waist and lifting me off my feet.

A giggle escapes me as I grab either side of his face and smother him in kisses. "You did great."

He somehow gives his signature smirk under the constant barrage of my affection. "Thank you, sweetheart. I missed you."

"It's been like two hours."

"Exactly. It felt like an eternity. Also, you owe me a back massage. Tammy asked five questions, not twelve. They all had a really good understanding of common safety knowledge and the concept of readiness bags."

I scoff, only slightly sad when he drops me lightly to my feet. "Well, it's probably because you've been teaching them about safe exits since kindergarten."

It's true. Once a year, Kam and the guys visit the elementary school and go over different things with the kids. James gets suited up and walks around so the smaller children get familiar with what they look like in all their gear. I hadn't understood why that mattered until Kam explained it.

If there's a fire, there's smoke, and if a young child gets separated from their parents and sees a huge figure walking toward them or searching, they may hide because they're scared.

"So what did Tammy ask?"

Kam shrugs, leaning back on the counter. He props his forearms on the edge near the papers for the carnival, and my heart skips. "Standard stuff. Wattage usage, LED light bulbs.

Epilogue

Why I want her to throw her computer out a third-story window."

I laugh at the way he words it, but even more so at the astounded look on Elise's face. "Why the hell would you want her to do that?"

"Because," I start, strategically turning to stand next to Kam and mirroring his stance. I'm able to move the file over a few inches inconspicuously with my elbow. "If the fire is in your hall, trapping you in, and you're on a high floor, the best thing to do is let the firefighters know where you are. You can't break the window because this will give the fire more oxygen, but if you open it momentarily to toss something out, they'll see the items and know people are stuck on that side. Which results in them getting to you faster."

Kam pulls me back into his arms, garnering a surprised gasp from me. "Look at my little volunteer trainee. I'm proud of you, sweetheart."

I beam at his words and nearly melt when he places a soft kiss on the tip of my nose.

"So, ready to tell me what booth you chose?"

"Ready to tell me yours?"

"Not a chance, sweetheart." He turns us both, keeping one of his arms slung over my shoulders as we walk out. "Guess we'll find out tomorrow."

I guffaw and shoot a quick wave to Elise. "Guess we will."

Along with what we're raising money for, Kam and I have been tight lipped about what our booths are. Part of me thinks he's going to do the funnel cakes again because of how massively successful they were, but the other part knows just how much he loves the idea of competing with me more.

He's got a guy, James, who can coax a honey jar from a bear, which leads me to believe he might have gotten some intel.

Epilogue

As we drive to the house, we converse as normal, but I can tell from the stiffness in his shoulders and his less than expansive conversation that something's wrong. Almost as if he's nervous. I want to ask, but I can bet my bottom dollar it's got something to do with the carnival.

Oh, I swear he's going to get it if we have the same booth again.

He pulls into the garage just as the sun kisses the horizon. The sky is colored in hues of pinks, blues, and purples, reminding me of the cotton candy I'll be serving tomorrow.

"About that massage." Kam opens the front door, allowing me to lead the way inside. "I'm thinking it can be after a couple of rounds with the kitty whip."

"You're going to try and flog the information out of me?" I push him off playfully. I know there's nothing he can do to get the information from me, but that damn flogger usually has me on my fucking knees, begging for release. Or laughing until I cry.

The man's a damn magician.

"Now why would I do something like that?" Kameron shoots me the smirk that makes his dimple pop. He pushes back his hair before motioning to the patio door. "Come see the sunset with me."

I roll my eyes, ignoring how my pussy clenches when he pulls me after him. "You'd do something like that because you're a dirty cheat."

He leads me through the back door before turning and tugging me flush against his chest. Gripping my chin with his thumb and forefinger, he lifts my face to look at him. "And you're my dirty little slut who *likes it* when I play dirty."

I can't argue there. "Fine. Massage after the flogger." I wave him off. "But I'm still not going to tell you what we're making, and I'm *definitely* going to win."

Epilogue

"That so?" He leans over and presses soft kisses across my jaw and down my neck. His touch is so light it sends shivers through me.

Still, I find my voice. "*Yep.*"

"Hmm," he hums, the deep sound vibrating across my chest, sending tingles over my skin.

In the next breath, pops of fireworks steal my attention. There's a small group of people over the lake who seem to be practicing for tomorrow. The long streams of light shoot high into the sky before exploding into the beautiful hues of color. The contrast against the sinking sun is breathtaking.

After another beat, Kam steals my mouth. The kiss is long and hungry, and the only reason we break apart is when we have to come up for air.

"How about a new wager, Firefly?" The blues in his eyes are dark and ominous, and for some reason, I get extremely excited for whatever challenge he's going to throw at me.

"And what would we be playing for?" I ask, though it's barely above a heady whisper.

He tilts his head toward the small bursts of light coming from the fireworks still illuminating our balcony with bright colors. I glance over, and it's then I see them. It's hard to make out every one, but the squad cars and fire trucks are an immediate giveaway that both our departments are lined up on the shore, holding sparklers in their hands.

I spin to ask Kam what's going on, but I'm answered with him on a single knee, a little black box in his hands.

"We'll play for keeps."

THE END.

Preview of Hollows Grove

Evelyn

How is it that best friends always find a way to rope you into shit that makes you question your sanity? That makes you contemplate how in the hell you've stayed friends for so long?

Ciara knows I'm scared of *literally* everything. She knows I don't do spiders bigger than my thumb, I can't look at a clown without almost shitting my pants, and the last time I saw a scary movie, I was thirteen. And I only watched it because I was tricked under the pretense that it was a parody.

These are never-changing facts that she's been privy to since we met in fifth grade. Yet, here I am, putting the finishing touches on my Halloween outfit for her murder mystery party.

One that I'm not only helping *host* but am also *participating* in.

One where I could be the victim.

Or even worse, *chased*. I could end up like all those clumsy, token characters in the movies and fall down a flight of stairs or run smack-dab into a tree. So many potential catastrophes, and all of which have my name on them.

The only pro in the extremely long list of cons is that she's having me play the role of the maid. I consider it the singular upside because if I'm going to be forced to run through a mansion and possibly fake murdered, I might as well look sexy as fuck doing it. Plus, there's always the off chance I get lucky and am paired with one of her hot coworkers, where we do less clue hunting and more body searches.

I check the tulle under my skirt one last time, making sure it's secure. I wanted to add a little oomph to my store-bought *hot maid uniform* and had to sew an extra layer of the itchy material into the waistband. But even knowing how incredible my legs will look in the outfit, my internal dread about the night doesn't ebb in the slightest.

I push out a heavy sigh. "I still can't believe you convinced me that this is a good idea. How the hell do I always let you talk me into stuff?"

My best friend turns, pushing one of her passion twists from her shoulder, and smirks. Her deep mauve lipstick is perfect for her role as *Lady Lavender* and pairs well with her pastel purple blouse. "Because in the almost twenty years we've known each other, there's nothing we won't do for one another."

I shake my head, twirling a loose string hanging from the bodice around my index finger and snap it off. "Yeah, but it's never involved being hunted down and murdered."

Normally, when I'm pulled into one of Ciara's shenanigans, it involves a random trip to an island, deep diving into her latest fling's social media, or staying up until four in the morning watching movies so she isn't lonely while she's doing her hair.

It's because of those same antics that I'm able to say I've

seen a good portion of the world, made it through a seven-year relationship that ended in a failed engagement, and live in a spider-free townhouse. You know, because she's my own personal eight-legged arachnid eradicator.

"You won't be hunted down." Ciara lets out an exasperated sigh as she flips through the manila envelopes on the kitchen island for the third time. "And I'm doing this because, with my new position at work, I really need to do some team building with the staff."

"Yeah, and I have to go, why?"

She huffs. "Because you're my girl, and I need you there in case it doesn't go perfectly."

My eyes roll so hard that a sharp ache radiates through the back of them. "Since when does anything you do *not* turn out perfectly?"

She blinks for a moment, looking as though she might actually be able to recall a time when she *didn't* obsess over every minute detail of something until it was flawless. Then, of course, when the inevitable happens and she comes back blank, she laughs. "You're being dramatic, Eve. The mansion is used for more than just Halloween events. Really, it's not even creepy."

My mouth gapes open as I slap a hand on the counter. The sharp noise echoes off the walls, and the pain shooting up my forearm makes me acutely aware of how hard granite is. "My ass! I saw the photos. They go all out for Halloween. That's not even *including* the surrounding woods and the cliff it's next to. At night, that place is the epitome of terrifying, Ciara."

"It's a wedding venue," she says a little too wearily as she slips the envelopes inside a large bag. "I don't get why you're still so sca—"

"Because of *your* brother," I hiss the obvious before she can finish. "And wedding venue? The only people getting married in that house on the hill are *The Addams Family* fanatics and ghost hunters."

"Again, you're being dramatic."

I hop down from the barstool I've been warming for half an hour and scoff as I stretch, "About which part? Your brother or the estate? Because I have irrefutable facts, some of which are decades old, as to how I'm not."

She narrows her eyes, but she knows she doesn't have a good rebuttal because the estate is so horrifying at night, it's been used in horror movies. Two of which were slashers where victims did, in fact, get run off the cliff.

She's also well aware that her brother is an asshole. At least, he is to me. Has been since I moved here when I was ten. It was shortly after my father decided staying together as a family wasn't worth it anymore, and split.

Most small-town people know that remaining there following a failed marriage is shit, which is why my mom and I moved to a new city in hopes of a fresh start.

Ciara and her family happened to be our next-door neighbors, and it didn't take more than a week of walking home from school together before I was at her house every day.

Soon after, the Davis family became part of mine. Mrs. Davis always sent me home with dinner, and since my mom was a nurse and didn't get home till almost eight, it was always a nice treat. On the weekends, Mr. Davis would help my mom with any issues around the house. Ciara's parents gave her the break she needed and peace of mind knowing I was cared for when she was at work.

Everything was perfect. It made the ache of missing my parents together seem almost nonexistent, and there was never a time when I longed for life before the divorce.

And it was all thanks to the Davis family. Well, three out of

Preview of Hollows Grove

the four. Ciara's older brother was a complete dick. The worst person imaginable. The splinter I could never get out.

He's three years older than Ciara and I, and man-oh-man, I wanted to deck him in the face on more than a dozen occasions.

At first glance, he's fucking hot. Like unbearably beautiful, with a smile that should be in every toothpaste commercial, and the personality of a humble jock who is just as smart as he is talented. If you asked anyone about him, they'd say he's the sweetest young man they've ever met, and how he wouldn't hesitate to give a stranger the shirt off his back.

But if you asked me? I'd say the complete opposite because, for some reason I still don't understand, he's got a fascination with scaring me.

It started with him putting fake bugs in my food and hiding around dark corners when I would stay the night. He did any and everything he could to get me to lose my shit.

When I asked him why, he said he enjoyed making me scream. He got the biggest kick out of it, and no matter how mad I got, it only made him want to do it more. Or do something worse.

One time, he stood over me when I was sleeping and just stared at me until I woke up and saw him hovering over me. After that, I don't think I got a good night's sleep until he left for college.

Hell, even then, I always double-checked doors and triple-checked under my bed.

I won't lie, though. There were times—albeit brief and fleeting—when I saw the guy everyone talked about. The sweetheart under the mask. There was even a time I entertained the thought of seeing in what other ways he could make me scream, but the idea vanished quicker than it came.

Now, even knocking on thirty, he still fucks with me, which

is why I actively try to avoid him. Which leads me to my current dilemma; we're helping Ciara host the event.

Together.

Yes. Not only do I have to endure an evening full of what goes bump in the night, but I'm doing it with the man who is the literal cause of my fear of the dark.

I glance back at Ciara, waiting for her to try and tell me I'm exaggerating about her brother or the estate.

After another moment, she purses her lips and moves them back and forth, the challenge to prove me wrong evident in her bright brown irises. But we both know the truth, and she rolls her eyes in defeat.

"Exactly," I chide, opening the refrigerator and taking out one of the Canadian sparkling waters. I swear these things have some type of addictive additive in them. "So now I have to ask, what did I do to deserve this punishment you're subjecting me to?"

"He's gonna know you took one." Ciara points, cleaning the rest of the papers off the island and ignoring my question.

"And? I think it's safe to say he owes me a few." I hold the drink up in a faux toast, only to immediately have it swiped away.

"Hey!" I whirl around, and I let out something that's supposed to resemble a gasp but ends up turning into a distorted snort when I see who it is.

Ciara's brother, Dorian—the bane of my existence, the gray hair standing out in my sea of brown waves, the itch I can't reach—stands two feet away from me and tips my water against his annoyingly perfect lips with a wink.

He's dressed in black joggers and a plain white shirt, yet the fit looks tailor-made, molding to a broad chest and narrow waist that meets muscular thighs. I swear his picture should be hanging outside of an athletic store window.

Dorian's dark eyes seem to shimmer under the kitchen light as he takes another heavy gulp before nodding toward me. "Thanks, E. I was parched."

"That was mine, you ass." I narrow my gaze, contemplating whether or not I should snatch it back. But he's had his mouth on it, and knowing him, he'll turn it into some kind of innuendo that just stirs up more shit. Aside from scaring me, he loves making me squirm because he knows I somehow still find him attractive.

It was probably that time I saw him save a cat from a tree outside his house. I mean, who actually does that? In his prom tux, no less. Or it could have been from the Halloween party five years ago. The one I'm still trying to forget to this day...

Yeah. It was probably then.

"Funny. I don't remember you asking me if you could have one." He takes yet another sip, and I curse my traitorous eyes from watching his throat roll with the action.

Of course, he catches me, and the light brown skin at the corner of his eyes wrinkles as he grants me a lopsided smirk.

I ignore the way my stomach does some unwarranted jerk that could easily be mistaken for gas and spin around, grabbing another bottle from the fridge. "I don't have to ask. Half the time, I'm the one who buys them when I go grocery shopping with your sister."

Dorian and Ciara live together in a townhouse four units down from me, so I'm over more often than I'm not. Luckily, Dorian is usually out of town scouting potential recruits for the university he coaches football for, so we rarely cross paths.

"Well, sunshine, you didn't buy these." He starts to reach for my glass, but the look on my face gives him pause. After a second, he relents and shrugs. "I spit in all of them anyway. Enjoy."

My fingers tense around the top before I twist it off. When

it doesn't crack from the safety seal separating, my internal debate over what I should do begins.

He's trying to call my bluff—something he does regularly—and scare me into bowing out. I don't particularly believe him, but I also don't really want to chug his saliva either.

Another moment passes, and I consider just letting him win this one, but the smug look on his face is reason enough not to care. I tip the glass back and take a heavy swig. The bubbles burn my throat on the way down, and the minute drop in his smirk is enough to make swallowing whatever might be in the bottle worth it.

Naturally, my triumph is short-lived.

"You like my spit in your mouth, sunshine?"

I almost choke on the water as Ciara makes a gagging sound that's a little too realistic. Slamming the glass on the island, I shoot him the bird. "Fuck off, Dorian."

He shrugs again, finishing his drink that's meant to be savored, and looks at his sister. "You regret this decision yet?"

"I did the moment I asked." Ciara sighs, tossing her bag over her shoulder as she shakes her head. "We leave in twenty, y'all, and for the love of God, please, *please*, be nice tonight. It's only like six hours of your entire life."

I throw a hand out. "It's him you need to be talking to."

Ciara is already halfway to the front door, but she stops to give me a look that says the words before she does. "You're just as petty, Eve. Do I need to remind you of the time you put cayenne pepper in his underwear?"

"Ciara!" I whirl around to see Dorian's mouth wide open.

I'd never admitted I did it, and in the end, he had to make a doctor's appointment because he thought he'd caught something from one of his hookups. I felt bad, but not bad enough to confess and face his wrath.

Dorian doesn't say anything for at least ten awkward

seconds as his eyes flit between me and her, before clamping his mouth shut. He nods more to himself than to us and grabs his keys off the counter, brushing past me without another glance.

"Y'all meet me in the car when you're ready."

I exchange a look with my best friend, whose mouthed 'sorry' does nothing to ease the flurry of anxiety testing out my heart muscle's dexterity.

Well, shit.

Acknowledgments

Thank you, my reader, for filling your time with the stories in my head.

As always, thank you to my hubs who made this book possible with wrangling the kids and cooking me yummy meals. To my kids for always walking in when I'm writing the spiciest scenes. And to my incredible alphas and betas.

Andrea, Dominique, Erica, Salma, Lily , M.L., Lo, Batool Zainab, and Garnet.

Y'all are the effing bomb and I hope you never leave me! Thank you for putting up with me being so last minute and needing everything done in one day. Like seriously. I love y'all.

Thanks to my amazingggggg beautifier. Mackenzie. Seriously. The back and forth, the long talks, the motivation and never-ending encouragement. Like you have no idea how confident you make me not only in putting my words out in the world but in myself in general. Thank you!

Ellie, for always fitting me in last minute! You always have so much going on, but you always come through in the clutch. Thank you!

And Ria, look at what you made girl!! I don't know how I got so lucky but are a gem!

Again, thank you to everyone! You beautiful people talked me into doing a Halloween Novella so subscribe to my newsletter or join my Facebook page to get the first look at tropes, covers, and more!

About the Author

Lee Jacquot is a wild-haired bibliophile who writes romances with strong heroines that deserve a happy ever after. When Lee isn't writing or drowning herself in a good book, she laughs or yells at one of her husband's practical jokes.

Lee is addicted to cozy pajamas, family games nights, and making tents with her kids. She currently lives in Texas with her husband, and three littles. She lives off coffee and Dean Winchester.

Visit her on Instagram or TikTok to find out about upcoming releases and other fun things! @authorleejacquot

Also by Lee Jacquot

I wrote a couple other books!! Check them out here!

Holinight Novellas
Christmas on the Thirteenth Floor
The Four Leaf
Liberty Falls
Hollows Grove

Wicked Wonderland Duet
Queen of Madness (Book 1)
King of Ruin (Book 2)

The Emerald Falls Series
The Masks We Wear
The Masks We Break
The Masks We Burn

Printed in Great Britain
by Amazon